ULTRA LOUNGE:
THE LEXICON OF EASY LISTENING

ULTRA LOUNGE:
THE LEXICON OF EASY LISTENING
BY DYLAN JONES

UNIVERSE

First published in the United States of America in 1997
by UNIVERSE PUBLISHING
A Division of Rizzoli International Publications, Inc.
300 Park Avenue South
New York, NY 10010

Designed by Robin Chevalier/Planet X

97 98 99/10 9 8 7 6 5 4 3 2 1

Printed and bound in Spain by Bookprint

Library of Congress Cataloging-in-Publication Data

Jones, Dylan.
    Ultra lounge : the lexicon of easy listening / by Dylan Jones.
        p.   cm.
    ISBN 0-7893-0095-8
    1. Popular music—History and criticism.   I. Title.
ML3470.J66   1997
781.64'09'04—dc21   96–52995
                                                        CIP
                                                        MN

For Doug, not least for 'Somewhere Down The Line'

Thanks to Steve Beard, John Bowers, Irwin Chusid, Andy Connell, Adrian Deevoy, Bill DeMain, Trevor Dolby, Corinne Drewery, Paul Du Noyer, Mark Ellen, Tony Elliott, Kodwo Eshun, Douglas Flett, Kathryn Flett, Pascal Gabriel, Helen Gallacher, Chris Gunning, Sally Holloway, Terry Jones, Cosmo Landesman, Nick Logan, Jim McClellan, Sean O'Hagan, Tony Parsons, Tony Peake, Kate Quarry, Robert Sandall, Alix Sharkey, Giles Smith, R.J.Smith, Mat Snow, David Toop, Sarah Walter, Colin Webb, and to Audrey and Mike for exposing me to Dean Martin at such an early age (so to speak).

Introduction
Lost In The Supermarket

The scene is from Carl Reiner's 1979 movie *The Jerk*. Steve Martin, as the adopted son of a poor black family in the Deep South, lying in bed one night – sad, lonely and completely alienated because of his inability to keep rhythm like his brothers and sisters – hears the saccharine strains of supermarket music coming from his grandma's battered old wireless. It hits him like a bolt from the blue. 'I've never heard music like this before!' he shrieks. 'It speaks to me! This is the kind of music which tells me to go out there and *be* somebody!'

Steve Martin had discovered the white man's blues, but even he wasn't quite sure what it was. Easy listening has always been a catch-all term, a holding bay for the kitsch, the maudlin and euphoric: soul ballads, torch songs and cabaret anthems; travelogue instrumentals, pop bossa nova and gleaming theme tunes. It has encompassed everything from Burt Bacharach and Dionne Warwick to Dean Martin and Hugo Montenegro; from John Barry, Nelson Riddle and Antonio Carlos Jobim to Barbra Streisand, Sandie Shaw and Matt Monro (the bus driver who became a hand-held torch singer). And God, as always, is in the details: easy demands swirling strings, piping-hot horns and extravagant keyboards – literally great washes of orchestration.

It is not only the sound. Easy listening is a world of possibilities, a virtual

The last, great, undiscovered Dionne Warwick album, tweaked – predictably – by Burt Bacharach

Our reluctance to grow up could explain why so much in modern easy listening concerns itself with travel – arrival, departure, perpetual motion; never being around means never having to say you're sorry exercise in perpetual freedom . . . life in the fast lane set to xylophone and flute. And in the departure lounge of 'lounge' (a place clothed – naturally – in leopard and sharkskin) there is room for the furious ultra nova of Marcos Valle, the idiosyncratic supperclub doo-wop of Tommy Edwards, the electronic wizardry of Louis and Bebe Barron, the dessert-wine-wafer-thin-mint-and-raging-gas-fire-soul of Dusty Springfield; room for torch singers, somnambulists and shriekers, crooners, swingers and lounge lizards; room for the audacious rhythms, staccato bursts, bewitching melodies and Gregorian cocktails of Xavier Cugat and Yma Sumac; the three-minute mini-movies and instrumental stylings of Roland Shaw and Henri René; room for the lush, innovative mixture of sounds produced by easy guru Juan Garcia Esquivel ('Juan Step Beyond!') – often referred to as the Mexican Duke Ellington, a Paganini for the jet set, the complete enchilada.

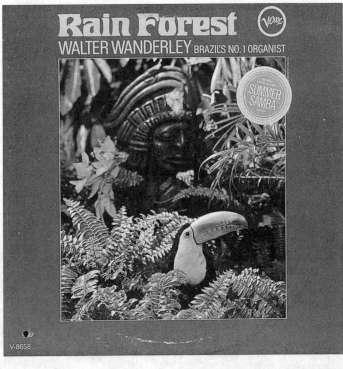

Walter Wanderley's wonderful rain forest crunch

There is room for brunch baroque, Mai-Tai melodies, space-age bachelor pad music, fusak (a mix of muzak and fusion), slumber music, pure pop (Alessi, Todd Rundgren, Michael Franks), elevator noir (particularly Brian Eno and Angelo Badalamenti), sonic wallpaper and moodsong as well as the easy-pop inventions of Swing Out Sister, St. Etienne and United Future Organisation.

'Before acid rock, there was cocktail music,' writes Joseph Lanza, the author of *Elevator Music*. 'But unlike its hippie counterpart, cocktail music never needed any pretences to Eastern mysticism to turn people on. Even its mind-altering substance was eminently legal. And like the drink, the music is a mixture of varying elements – equal parts show tunes, jazz, polka, Pacific Island love songs, ballroom ballads, playful rock and even a dash or two of folk.'

In some form or another, this music has been with us for the best part of the twentieth century – in dance halls and ballrooms, on the radio, on living-room Dansettes the world over; when Nixon was inaugurated, muzak was broadcast from loudspeakers on Capitol Hill, while Buzz Aldrin and Neil Armstrong even listened to easy sounds on their Apollo lunar cruise. It is now part of history, as Lanza points out. To wit: on 28

July, 1945, a B-25 bomber crashed into the Empire State Building's seventy-ninth storey. The elevator shafts caught fire, while fifty people were trapped inside a glass observatory on the eighty-eighth floor. The following day's *New York Post* reported that, 'even at this terrifying juncture, the "canned" music that is wired into the observatory continued to play, and the soothing sounds of a waltz helped the spectators there to control themselves. There was no panic . . .'

Good scenery deserves a decent soundtrack, music which can add more than pathos to the magical vista in front of us – music that can

Glass Walls   *Dust-free Floors*   *Menu Selector*   *Gl*
                                                    and Microwave Stove

complement the feeling (real, or imagined) of careering around the Amalfi coast in an open-top sports car, conjure up images of sharp-suited secret agents cavorting about in Portmeirion, Monaco or the Florida Keys, or simply evoke the languor of a moonlight tropical beach ('Two views for every boy!'). Easy listening is that music, a passport to international listening pleasure, a soundtrack for life; to paraphrase one *aficionado*, the easy-listening fan can drive to the shops like anybody else, but with the right Percy Faith track on the stereo he does it in split-screen Technicolor, in a Maserati, accompanied by glockenspiel, clave and marimba. From

Here in our Polynesian Populuxe dreamworld, prosperity and convenience surround us ('Jeez, this chaise longue has tail-fin arms!'), as do the stabbing saxophones, angular banjos, swirling Moogs, giddy basslines and gorgeous intrusions of massed violins

ILLUSTRATED BY FRED McNABB

uit
Ultrasonic Laundry

Electrical Heat Unit
Phono-vision Receiver

the dream lounge and the waiting-room to the production line, from the supermarket to the atrium – an escape to Martiniland. 'I always tried to make songs that were mini-movies,' said Burt Bacharach once, as though aural picturesque travelogues were the most natural thing on earth.

In its own way the genre has always offered a respite from reality, a sense of completeness, a return to the womb . . . But in every dream home there is a heartache. Easy, the eternal slur, is a misnomer. Bacharach and Hal David's compositions, for example, are anything but: little epiphanies that they were, they could be deceiving, and though many of their songs were snapshots of sunny prosperity, there was often heavy pathos hovering just behind the sun deck; David's words full of heartbreak, Bacharach's convoluted music never less than maudlin. In Isaac Hayes's hands, for example, Bacharach's songs are deconstructed, decoded and dismantled to such an extent that they become different songs altogether, held together only by the melody. Listening to Hayes tackle 'The Look Of Love' for the first time puts you in mind of Sinead O'Connor's version of 'Nothing Compares 2U', or Whitney Houston's 'I Will Always Love You'. Hardly easy.

The Four King Cousins: it's pop, Jim, but not as we know it

'Atmospheric, inextricably intertwined with movie music, easy listening transported its audience to a better place than grim reality, while at the same time indulging our emotions,' writes Paul Staheli. 'You could wallow in it, revel in the romance and ache at the pain, and though many of the vocalists, male and female, were unabashed drama queens, it wasn't just the words that made you shiver. Next time you're feeling lonely, stick on "Anyone Who Had A Heart", the Dionne Warwick version. Brilliantly manipulative, it pulls at all the right strings, making your bottom lip tremble along to a crescendo that makes you bawl. Easy listening takes you where self-conscious rock and pop fear to tread.'

But, easy or not, it was the stuff of personal obsession, not nationwide – certainly not global – attention. Until recently, that is.

If, in 1989, someone had offered to pay you a substantial amount of money to predict what would happen to pop culture over the next ten years, what would you have suggested? Morphed movie stars? CD-Rom wrist watches? Internet sex? Surely a re-appreciation of Burt Bacharach couldn't have been further from your mind. Until recently easy listening was largely ignored by pop consumers and critics alike, always considered the poor relation in an extended family that contains jazz, pop, rock, country, blues and all the rest. And when it was appreciated, it was almost always from a camp perspective (how many 'serious' music consumers are there who express an ironic penchant for Abba or the Carpenters?). The buzzwords surrounding the genre were hardly complimentary, and included such pejorative terms as quasi, ersatz, kitsch, mock, corny etc. Music Lite, even.

For years easy listening was the most critically neglected music in the world, a music so maligned you could have been forgiven for assuming it had been responsible for some form of global genocide. Pop music has dominated the charts since the fifties, pushing MOR (Middle Of the Road), the pop of the previous generation, into the margins. Consequently this made it the most marginal music of our time, and the Sandpipers, Nat 'King' Cole, Laurie Johnson and Tony Christie seemed

In our own exotic ranch-style place – reachable only by a two-door supersonic Firedrome convertible or a Skyway jet – *The Love Machine* is rarely off the turntable, Donald Fagen rarely off the piano; Danny Williams holds court by the pool as Walter Wanderley and Corinne Drewery attempt the perfect Martini

'Where Are You Now'? 'Somewhere Down The Line'? 'Joanna'? 'I Can't Tell The Bottom From The Top'? 'Downtown'? 'Boy Blue'? A songwriting summit, with Jackie Trent, Tony Hatch, Guy Fletcher and Douglas Flett

destined to languish in the charity shops of this world, nestling between the bad career moves of REO Speedwagon and Hazel O'Connor.

There were, however, a few places where you could find the white man's blues. Almost all the old airlines seemed oblivious to the fads and fancies of the earth below, and played continuous easy-style sounds on their headphones as part of the in-flight entertainment. Some restaurants tried to keep the world at bay, too, and in breakfast bars and steak houses the world over, piped MOR would always be there for you. Hotels were once particularly adept at making you feel as though time had stopped after *Young at Heart,* and North American elevators are still a good source. Unfortunately, the one place where you'd expect to still find the good groove – the supermarket – is nowadays almost completely bereft of easy listening, or anything approximating it. Sainsbury's don't appear to be interested in the dulcet tones of Jack Jones, the hypermarkets of France pump out seamless Eurodisco, while the US prefers urban contemporary – leaving Ray Ventura, Dino and Dave Grusin out in the carpark.

Five years ago the death of MOR was considered a forgone conclusion, but these days, not a day goes by when something is not revived; it might be a crime writer, a fashion statement, an architectural movement, even a decade. These days it's impossible to let bygones be bygones. Look through any newspaper supplement and you'll be told that – bloody hell, *already!* – minimalism is back, or the platform shoe, or the forties, or the sixties, or – with increasing regularity – even the eighties. Popular culture, by its very nature, is blessed with built-in obsolescence, but today it comes complete with its own revival button, too. Press once to consign it to oblivion, press twice to bring it back.

In the world of fashion – where lasting statements are scarce – re-invention, revivals and homages are commonplace. 'Fashion used to do one decade at a time, but now they're all playing simultaneously,' says Sarah Mower from *Harper's Bazaar*. 'You can be Joan Crawford Monday, Audrey Hepburn Tuesday, Sophia Loren Wednesday, Marilyn Monroe Thursday, Jackie O Friday.' Or, alternatively, Cary Grant on Monday, Brian Jones Tuesday, Elliot Gould Wednesday, Burt Bacharach Thursday and – if you're particularly sad – Tony Hadley on Friday.

Bacharach is hardly a surprising choice. Sergio Mendes and Herb Alpert might have been masters of the aural sunset, yet for some their Latino style was a little too ersatz; Ray Coniff and Ray Davies (of the Button Down Brass) were always just a little too whitebread; while Esquivel and Martin Denny were not exactly fashion pin-ups. No, it was Bacharach who had the jet-set cool: the looks, the urbane sophistication, the cars and the girls. He personified the sixties bachelor, a man whose life actually mirrored those of the characters you saw in the movies. If Brian Wilson and Phil Spector were the kings of the dashboard radio, then Bacharach was the ruler of the open-plan hi-fi, a man who pushed fifties mood music into tomorrow. If Kennedy was your president, then Bacharach was your composer.

And on top of all this – and the reason that Bacharach was noticed in the first place – was the fact that he wrote like an eiderdown dream; with lyricist Hal David creating dozens of modern-day standards that are up there with anything by Porter, Gershwin or Berlin. As Julie Burchill wrote in *The Face* in January 1988, in a piece entitled 'Walk On By: the Songs of Burt Bacharach and the Decline of the American Orgasm': 'Across the pond, on the first day God created man and woman; on the second, the vodka martini, and on the third, the music of Burt Bacharach. And then on the fourth, man created rock and roll and ruined everything.'

If Hal David used the iconography of the sixties like his own private

Atmospheric, inextricably intertwined with movie music, easy listening transported its audience to a better place than grim reality, while at the same time indulging our own particular emotions. You could wallow in it, revel in the romance and ache at the pain

alphabet, then Bacharach painted a world which allowed it all to happen, creating great washes of sound that, during that period, eclipsed the work of many soundtrack composers. Bacharach's music was the music of a bright new dawn, a diffused modernist dream world which consisted of little more than neo-Polynesian cocktail bars and Sante Fe adobes surrounded by palm, cypress and bougainvillaea; the soundtrack of a time when Coke was still glamorous, when the future held only progress. Speeding along the great suburban highways of sunshine superland, a Bacharach symphony was all you needed.

'Unlike the other brilliant creatures of the Brill Building, Bacharach had played be-bop, studied classical and worked for Marlene Dietrich,' says Burchill. 'He was a pre-pop man who called to the aid of the pop song gospel, jazz and most of the *baoin*, the rhythm of Brazil, an irregular, rolling beat that played sharp to samba's sweetness. Allying white tunes with black structures and Latin rhythm, he created the perfect pop sound which, incredibly, was called "anarchic" and "iconoclastic" by critics. Ah, if only the Sex Pistols had sounded so good.'

Now sixty-eight, Bacharach seems a little bemused by this current attention. 'I'm finding out it's much more than I thought,' he says. 'It makes me very happy, though. I appreciate being appreciated.' The man still appears in cabaret – often with Dionne Warwick, with whom he famously fell out in the seventies – although he spends most of his time breeding racehorses. The past is not Bacharach's bag. 'It's like anything,' he says. 'If you're a tennis player and you're at a certain level, you have to play every day. It's not something you can pick up every three months.'

The recent vogue for all things lounge amongst London's after-dark élite is proof positive that what goes around comes around. Lounge (or 'Easy', 'Easycore', whatever) broke, as it were, in 1994, when Bacharach, Denny, Webb *et al* began being fêted at various central London nightclubs (*kitschpalaste* such as the World of Cheese, Indigo, Sound Spectrum, the Continental, etc.) and by several in-the-style-of bands including in Britain,

the Gentle People and Count Indigo; in the US, Combustible Edison; and in Japan, the Pizzicato Five.

Suddenly the sonic swirls and aural landscapes created by orchestral wizards like John Barry, Alan Moorehouse and Henry Mancini were flavour of the month, while the so-called nightlife *cognoscenti* began sporting mutton-chop sideburns, lime-green flares and jacket lapels wider than the jackets themselves. If, during the eighties, Herb Ritts was a name to drop, in the early nineties it was more likely to be Herb Alpert. It was a veritable Cocktail Nation.

There was a ground swell of support, and an amateur hour homage turned into a thriving cottage industry, as record companies from Harlesden to Seattle started banging out 'Cheesey Listening' CD compilations of everyone from Mantovani, Lawrence Welk, Keith Mansfield and Peter Nero to Shirley Bassey, Brian Fahey, the 101 Strings and the Three Suns (those fifties iconoclasts who mixed skating-rink music with light, orchestral coffee-coloured jazz). Noel Gallagher included Bacharach's photograph on the cover of the first Oasis LP ('If I could write a song as good as "This Guy's In Love With You" or "Anyone Who Had A Heart", I'd die a happy man,' he said), while Elvis Costello, Paul Weller, Bjork, Prince, Michael Stipe, Jarvis Cocker and dozens of other notable pop personages pledged their finger-clicking allegiance to the bri-nylon

Bacharach's appearance on the cover of the first Oasis LP was prescient: it was somewhat inevitable that Noel Gallagher should one day duet with Burt Bacharach, though that didn't make it any less extraordinary when it did eventually happen. And, unlike the rather gushy and irritating pastiches produced by the likes of Mike Flowers, you could tell that, should Gallagher ever cover one of the great man's songs, he would treat it with the utmost respect

flag (Gallagher sang 'This Guy's In Love With You' at Bacharach's first British concert in over thirty years at the Royal Festival Hall in June 1996). There were even new magazines, *Lounge* and *Easy*.

Now, no hip-hop tenement opera or paean to mail-order youth culture is complete without a knowing glance towards the eccentric orchestration of Bert Kaempfert, Billy May or Webley Edwards. Vic Damone? Top man. Lani Hall? Wonderful woman. John Gregory, Charles Stepney and Free Design? Sold to the man in the plasticine boots and lead trilby . . .

'Young renegades, tired of the constraints that the style police imposed on the generation before them, made their own anti-fashion statement,' said *Billboard*, 'focusing on the mock sophistication and nerdy image that the cocktail Latin style brought with it. Safari suits and crimpolene turtleneck sweaters are worn without shame. *The Avengers* re-runs on TV are gaining cult audiences, garish seventies plastic furniture is being aped by new designers, and James Bond and his leggy assistants are once again role models for a generation.'

The sophisticated schmaltz and beguiling soundscapes designed by mood masters such as Esquivel and Les Baxter have not only created a credible lineage for the perpetrators of modern ambient and trance music – from Stereolab to Stock, Hausen & Walkman – but newcomers to the great lost genre also developed their own musical language, one now employed by British bands as diverse as the Divine Comedy (pretentious art school muzak) and Corduroy (breathless Sergio Mendes pastiches), and by the successful easycore DJs James and Martin Karminsky. 'There's a fusion that opens up doors for a lot of things to be acceptable for home listening,' says club promoter Pete Lawrence. 'We have DJs

Lift-off! In some form or another, this music has been with us for the best part of the twentieth century – in dance halls and airports, on the radio, on living-room Dansettes the world over; when Nixon was inaugurated muzak was broadcast from loudspeakers on Capitol Hill, while Buzz Aldrin and Neil Armstrong even listened to easy sounds on their Apollo lunar cruise

who go from experimental techno to classical. Eclecticism is the key.'

And then there is Mike Flowers, a man who didn't so much re-invent the genre as pick it up and tickle it under the arms, exploiting its popularity by sending his own, quite extraordinary version of Oasis's 'Wonderwall' to the top of the British singles chart during Christmas 1995. As *Mojo* pointed out at the time, 'We have seen the future of rock and roll and it costs 19/11d.'

The main drawback with the genre's new-found popularity is that both consumers and musicians look suspiciously like they're changing the way they feel about it because every other form of music has now been re-activated, re-assessed and put on display in Tower Records, and Bacharach, Jackie Trent, Johnny Pearson and High Hollander seem only to have been resurrected from the cultural grave because practically everything else has been done. Blue beat, country, punk, heavy metal, glam and futurism had all been recalled from the pop-cultural skip, so why not lo-fi MOR?

Rotary Connection: the best-kept secret in the loungecore canon

There was a period just after punk broke in Britain when young bands were falling over themselves to pick their way through pop's recent past, reinventing themselves using everything from sixties power pop and plastic dresses to constructivist graphics and camouflage trousers; groups became industrial merchants of doom, *Thunderbird* puppets, urban loners and blue-collar academics (if you were Wire, Pere Ubu, the Pop Group or ABC, you had to have a good story to tell; the music was nothing if it wasn't contextualized). Ska, soul, disco, heavy rock – everything came back in all-too regular four-month cycles. Having exhausted most of the immediate past, easy's new-found popularity perhaps exposes the public's prolonged apathy towards a style of music that they thought was beyond redemption. Now, as eclecticism becomes a career, easy listening is just another victim of the post-modern blender, a part of the pop cultural loop.

It is a loop which contains more than music. Albert Goldman used to like to say that pop music was a way of staying young, a refusal to grow up, a way of keeping your world around you as you push on in life. Extreme, perhaps, though his views wouldn't be out of place amongst those being put forward by Robert Bly and Gail Sheehy, who both published works in 1996 identifying a trend towards 'half-adulthood'. Bly, author of *Iron John,* poet and founder of the 'Men's Movement', explored a Peter Pan syndrome in *The Sibling,* a book which argued that American – and by extension, Western – culture has created a society bereft of credible authority figures, a theory backed by *Vanity Fair* journalist Sheehy. 'Adolescence is now prolonged for the middle classes until the

19

end of the twenties,' she wrote. 'True adulthood does not begin until thirty.' Fifty years of pop consumption has had strange side effects, and as we get older we seem loathed to exchange the freedom of youth for the supposed domesticity of middle age. The *Observer*'s Peter Beaumont goes further, 'While childhood is ending earlier (pace *Kids*), adults are prolonging adolescence into their thirties. Many are not acknowledging their maturity until they hit forty. By some curious process of post-modern metrication, the seven ages of man have been devalued into three.'

This reluctance to grow up could explain why so much in modern easy listening concerns itself with travel – arrival, departure, perpetual motion: never being around means never having to say you're sorry. But over-analysation of pop (and pop culture) is a growth industry, clouding what is often just a combination of circumstance and time. It also tends to deny the remarkable life-affirming power of music, and its ability to make both happiness and sadness seem almost confrontational.

Which is, after all, why we're here, right now. As the writer Jim Irvin said of the Walker Brothers, '[They] achieved an irresistible blend of melancholy and optimism. They made the statement "My ship is coming in" seem ineffably sad and the assertion that "The sun ain't gonna shine any more" supremely uplifting. Their records understood that emotions are illogical and treacherous.'

Scott Walker understood – along with Jimmy Webb, Burt Bacharach, John Barry, Brian Wilson and all the rest – that music is not only too important to be treated lightly, but also, when the occasion demands it, too important not to be.

At the cocktail party of our dreams, they will all be there, along with Les Baxter, Nancy Sinatra, Viv Damone, Rotary Connection, Free Design and the Four King Cousins. In our own exotic ranch-style space-place – reachable only by a two-door supersonic Firedrome convertible or a Skyway jet – *The Love Machine* is rarely off the turntable, Donald Fagen rarely off the piano; Danny Williams holds court by the pool as Walter Wanderley and Corinne Drewery attempt the perfect martini.

Here in our Polynesian Populuxe dreamworld high above the city, prosperity and convenience surround us ('Jeez, this chaise longue has tail-fin arms!'), as do the stabbing saxophones, angular banjos, swirling Moogs, giddy basslines and gorgeous intrusions of massed violins. Here, in our *faux*-frontier fantasyland, night closes in, the moon casts extravagant shadows on the street below, and the robotic fizz of canned laughter crawls from the TV.

Walking slowly towards the kitchen, you pick up *The Very Best Of Martin Denny*. 'Listen,' it commands on the sleeve, 'if you hold the album cover up to your ear you can hear the sea.' So you do. And indeed you can.

Herb Alpert

If history can be caught in a single breath, then there are few better ways of explaining the Populuxe aspirations of American suburbia during the late fifties and early sixties (when the advertising industry began to believe its own publicity) than by listening to the piercing yet sweet 'Ameriachi' sound of Herb Alpert and his Tijuana Brass.

As the fifties gave way to the sixties, the suburban soundtrack of Mai-Tai melodies and Space-age bachelor pad music (a kind of homely filter-tipped sonic wallpaper) was displaced by the brash, urban sophistication of men like Burt Bacharach, Sergio Mendes and Herb Alpert. As teen idols replaced the gruff rock'n'roll greaseballs, so smart young band leaders replaced the quirkier exponents of 'Exotica'. Alpert in particular credits the delirious, happy sound of the Tijuana Brass with ushering in a new era of American pop. 'It's not a protest and not a put-down,' he says. 'I think people were bugged with hearing music which had an undercurrent of unhappiness and anger, even sadism.'

In the beginning, it was all serendipity. Born in Los Angeles in 1935 into a musical family (his father played the mandolin, his mother the violin, his sister the piano and his brother the drums), Alpert took up the trumpet at the tender age of eight, later studying with jazz and classical tutors at Fairfax High School. After two years in the Army as a trumpeter-bugler at San Francisco's Presidio garrison, he worked in LA as an A&R man, record producer, composer (writing 'Wonderful World', amongst others, for Sam Cooke) and session musician. He was a Herb of all trades.

One day in 1962, messing about in his ad-hoc studio in the garage next to his house, he began experimenting with a song called 'Twinkle Star' which had been written by a friend of his, Sol Lake. Exploiting the tune's Spanish flavour, Alpert came up with a version that had some of the intonations of Mexican mariachi music; and so 'The Lonely Bull', the Tijuana Brass and A&M Records (hastily organized with another friend, record promotion man Jerry Moss) were born. Herb Alpert's Tijuana Brass became the South of the Border soundtrack of the swinging sixties, flashpointed in 'Casino Royale', 'Tijuana Taxi', 'Spanish Flea' and 'A Taste of Honey'; while by 1968 A&M's annual turnover was in excess of $50 million, helped by the success of the Sandpipers and Sergio Mendes. During the seventies and eighties Alpert concentrated on running his record company, occasionally popping up with funk and dance tracks such as 'Rise', 'Rotation' (both 1979) and 'Keep Your Eye On Me' (1987).

For all his talk of giddy pop, Alpert is a master at moodsong, and his haunting trumpet sound has an innate maudlin quality. To wit: 'There are some things which have definitely sad overtones, like the tune we wrote in memory of the matador, Carlos Arruza, who was such a big influence

Co-founder of A&M Records, Alpert has sold more instrumental albums than almost any other performer in history. 'I just hit on this idea of using a mariachi sound together with American jazz,' he says, plainly. 'I was playing like I felt – and I still do to this day.'

upon my whole idea for the Brass sound. He was fighting in Tijuana on the day I got the inspiration for the sound. Thinking of how tragically he died, in a head-on automobile collision, after fighting bulls for twenty-five years, that music didn't come out too happy.'

classic

Herb Alpert & the Tijuana Brass
'Casino Royale' (2.37)
Single (A&M) 1967
The ex-Army trumpeter's blistering version of Bacharach and David's theme from the Bond-spoof movie starring David Niven, Peter Sellers and Woody Allen. Alpert's quasi-Mexican sound was never as pertinent as it is here, and the horns were never so shrill.

classic

The Art of Noise
'Robinson Crusoe' (3.49)
Album: The Best Of The Art Of Noise (China) 1992
A faithful recreation of the sixties television theme which welds a modern (at least in the mid-eighties) drum sound to the sentimental strains of the ultimate desert island disc. Quaint, eerie and mildly disturbing, this record is also surprisingly uplifting.

'Asteroids'
'One of the most reliable methods for writers to make a fool of themselves in print is to try to spell a tune,' wrote Jonathan Margolis in the *Sunday Times*. ' "Bum bum ti bum booo bah," we prattle, when trying to describe some well-known theme without the benefit of being able to hum it. If I hit you with this one, however – go on, just one more try, please – you might just get it: "Pa-paa pa-paa pa-paa pa-paa pa-pa-pa, Pa-paa pa-paa pa-paa pa-paaa pa," it starts. Got it?'

Of course you have. Pearl & Dean's notorious advertising jingle has become a mantra for British cinema-goers since its creation twenty-eight years ago. It is so well known that Pearl & Dean believe their logo is known for its sound rather than its image. People sing it on entering the cinema, sing along with it when they eventually hear it, and even leave singing it. So cherished is this blistering space-age ident that one Welsh cinema manager arranged to have it played at his own cremation, as his coffin slid behind the curtains.

Written in 1968 by the forty-two-year-old composer Peter Moore in his house in Acton, 'Asteroids' was recently re-recorded by the Wolverhampton pop group Goldbug and welded on to a cover version of Led Zeppelin's 'Whole Lotta Love', becoming a huge hit in the process. 'We went to see *Terminator 2* and realized we were all looking forward to the Pearl & Dean music,' says Goldbug member Richard Walmsley. 'But it didn't happen. It was just not there. And that got us thinking. "Asteroids" is music that speaks to your darkest regions.'

Burt Bacharach
by Bill DeMain

It's summer 1957 at 49th and Broadway in New York City, inside a building whose hallways are vibrating with an inspired cacophony. There are eleven floors of offices here, most of them home to music publishing companies. In each one songwriters are making a living, pounding on piano keys, scratching words on legal pads, stomping out beats. Voices wail, waiver, pause, confer for a moment, laugh, then wail some more.

The sound of pop music being born.

This is the Brill Building, Manhattan's musical marketplace of talent, tunes and deals. In its stuffy cubicles, just about big enough for a piano and two chairs, some of the greatest ampersands of song – Goffin & King, Barry & Greenwich, Sedaka & Greenfield and Mann & Weil – will huddle together in the early sixties to hammer out the songs that will connect with each succeeding generation. But right now, in one of these sonic saunas two not-yet-famous songwriters, both New Yorkers, both dressed in the *de rigueur* uniform of the day – white button-down shirt, skinny black tie – are working together for the first time.

The composer is Burt Bacharach. A staffer for Famous Music Publishing, he's an athletic all-American with thick, wavy hair and the kind of bone structure more commonly found yachting on the Hamptons than gnomishly bent over a Brill Building piano. (Sammy Cahn later said, 'Burt's the only songwriter who doesn't look like a dentist.') He has trained

Top: There is enigmatic, and then there is enigmatic. The Art of Noise – forgivably, we think – were definitely enigmatic. Or something

Bottom: By the way, which one's Dean? The problem with Pearl & Dean's magnificent theme tune is that invariably the ads that follow are always something of a let-down. After all, how could they possibly not be?

his ear to some unusually *outré* sounds – Dizzy Gillespie and be-bop jazz, Debussy – influences further refined to mould his unique style by years of study at the Mannes School of Music with renowned composition teacher Darius Milhaud ('he told me to never be afraid of writing a tuneful melody,' says Burt today). He's been around the globe working as an arranger and accompanist for vocalists Vic Damone, Steve Lawrence and, most prominently, Marlene Dietrich. He also has one minor hit to his name – 'The Blob', a horror flick tie-in for The Five Blobs. This was co-written with successful Tim Pan Alley songsmith Mack David who introduced Burt to his younger brother, Hal. A soft-spoken New Yorker with a sweet-natured grin, Hal wrote the lyrics to a few minor hits including 'American Beauty Rose' and 'Bell Bottom Blues', and has earned enough clout to be working on a song-by-song basis with a number of different publishers.

'You'd write with one composer in the morning and another in the afternoon,' Hal David, now seventy-four, recalls. 'I met Burt, we liked each other, we liked the songs he wrote and that's how it began. We worked hard – I was always writing lyrics, he was always writing melodies. We'd meet around eleven o'clock every day: "What do you think of this? What do you think of that?" Either my lyric would spark him to write a melody or vice versa.'

'It was a smoke-filled room with a window that didn't open and a beat-up piano,' muses Burt Bacharach. 'Your typical image of how songwriters wrote in those days.'

And they were very prolific.

'As we were working together on one song, he'd give me another melody or I'd give him another lyric, and very often we were writing three or four songs at a time,' Hal David remembers. 'A song together, a song to his tune, a song to my lyric and so forth. We kept a number of things going.'

Once one of those things was finished the duo would hawk their wares. 'There were eleven floors in the Brill Building and you'd start at the top and work your way down,' chuckles Hal.

The wares of Bacharach and David, even in those first years, were strikingly different from the work of the teenybop-oriented competition. The music had a sophistication you would not encounter in the formulaic fare of the late fifties. It married unexpected rhythms with daring melodic leaps; it shimmered with rich jazz-like changes and complex harmonies; it teased with its uneven form and challenged with its mild yet exotic dissonance. And of course, at first, it didn't fly with record company types.

'All those so-called abnormalities seemed perfectly normal to me,' says Bacharach, today a tanned and trim sixty-eight. 'In the beginning, the A&R guys, who were like first lieutenants, would say, "You can't dance to it" or "That bar of three needs to be changed to a bar of four", and

'I don't try to break the rules consciously, because most of them come from a harmonic source,' . says Bacharach. 'It just happens. Like, we were finishing a song with Dionne once and she was counting the eighth-note flow. She said, "Gee, this only comes to seven notes." So we did it as a 7/8 bar. It felt good that way'

because I wanted to get the stuff recorded I listened and ended up ruining some good songs. I've always believed if it's a good tune people will find a way to move to it.'

The lyrics matched to those tunes were equally unusual: they were grown-up. Hal David focused on adult affairs and described all the jealousy, vulnerability, longing and loneliness that comes with the territory. He quietly lists the three qualities he's always sought in his lyrics: 'Believability. Simplicity. Emotional impact.'

Despite their fair share of flops, the team proved themselves with a pair of back-to-back hits in 1958 – 'Magic Moments' by Perry Como and 'The Story Of My Life' by Marty Robbins (a hit in the UK for Michael Holliday). This was enough to hush the Brill Building doubters and encourage the duo to continue their collaboration.

But for the next three years, Burt and Hal worked together only intermittently. Bacharach wrote 'Any Day Now', 'Mexican Divorce' and big hit 'Tower of Strength' with lyricist Bob Hilliard; collaborating with Mack David and Barney Williams, he penned the Shirelles' classic 'Baby It's You', and he moonlighted as an arranger for the Drifters on songs such as '(Don't Go) Please Stay' and 'In The Land Of Make Believe'. David meanwhile provided words for various tunes, including Henry Mancini's 'Baby Elephant Walk', 'You'll Answer To Me' a hit for Patti Page, and Joanie Summer's minor classic 'Johnny Get Angry'. Then in 1962 fate brought the two maverick songwriters the perfect voice in the fetching shape of a young New Jersey session singer named Maria Dionne Warrick.

Bacharach discovered Dionne when she, her sister DeeDee and their Aunt Cissy [Houston] – known as the Gospelaires – were adding background vocals to the Drifters' version of 'Mexican Divorce'. 'She had pigtails and dirty white sneakers,' Burt recalled in 1970, 'and she just shone. The group was dynamite but there was something about the way she carried herself that made me want to hear her sing by herself. After I did, she started to do all our demos.'

The enchanting sound of the twenty-one-year-old's voice on a demo of 'It's Love That Really Counts' caught the ear of Scepter Records owner Florence Greenberg, and Dionne was quickly signed. Her first choice for a single was Bacharach and David's 'Make It Easy On Yourself' for which she'd done the demo.

When the authors told her that the song had already been recorded by Jerry Butler, so the story goes, Dionne, feeling betrayed, shouted, 'Don't make me over, man' (as in 'Don't try to con me'). By the time she'd cooled down a few days later, Burt and Hal had written her first single, the dramatic – you guessed it – 'Don't Make Me Over'. ('She had to sing an octave and a sixth on that,' Burt said, 'and she did it with her eyes closed.') When the ballad was pressed, a Scepter printing error made Dionne Warrick over into Dionne Warwick.

Her.voice was a sensitive, soulful instrument with an incredible dynamic range that enabled her to whisper with the demure intimacy of Julie London or soar with the gospel bravado of Aretha Franklin. And she understood nuance like few others. Where other vocalists stumbled awkwardly over a Bacharach melody (even Sinatra couldn't quite negotiate the bumpy terrain of 'Wives And Lovers'), she floated nimbly, easily accommodating odd bars in 5/4, digging deep in all the right places and perfectly conveying the ache and tenderness of David's poignant lyrics. 'Even back then, she had elegance, grace and the ability to sing just about anything,' states Bacharach, who toured the US in the summer of 1995 with Dionne. 'And as she grew, we were able to take more chances as writers.'

Their startling growth paralleled that of the Beatles, the Beach Boys and the Motown crowd, encapsulating the experimental spirit of the times: check out the smooth bossa strut of 'Walk On By' (Burt was an ardent admirer of Brazilian composers Antonio Carlos Jobim and Milton Nascimento), the tympani-pounding glory of 'Reach Out For Me', the breathless hormonal rush of 'I Say A Little Prayer', the intricate spiral staircase of a melody on 'Alfie' and the ambitious dynamic shifts of the often-overlooked 'Check Out Time' – these rank as some of pop's most exhilarating moments.

New York City, late summer 1966: Gary Chester is exploding in the bridge again. In the control room at A&R Studio A-1, 799 7th Avenue at 52nd Street, young engineer Phil Ramone eases down the drum levels.

'I can't hear anything else!' he laughs. The string mikes are picking up too much of Chester's ballistic playing. Burt likes it when Gary lets go and takes their songs to a new level, but, for some reason, this one isn't happening. Perhaps it's because the team's unofficial mascot, Phil's mom, isn't in her usual spot at the back of the control room, knitting and nodding her approval.

'I don't know, we seem to have peaked,' says Ramone. Hal David looks up from his book and raises an eyebrow at Phil who goes to find Bacharach conferring with backing singers Cissy Houston and DeeDee Warwick.

Seated back at the console, Ramone makes an adjustment to the Scully four-track, lights up a tall Marlboro 100 and smiles at Burt.

'If I didn't love you, I wouldn't sit next to you with this stuff,' Bacharach laughs.

'Why don't you play piano on this one, Burt?' asks the engineer.

'Aw, damn I don't want to,' sighs Bacharach.

'C'mon man, you have to play,' cajoles Ramone.

Reluctantly, Burt settles at the keyboard.

'OK, let's try it,' says Ramone over the talkback. '"I Just Don't Know What To Do With Myself" – take ten.'

Bacharach looks over at Gary Chester, nods, swings his right arm and clicks his fingers in a count-off. Bassist Russ Savakus falls in. This time the groove locks. Everyone – eighteen musicians, four singers and Dionne – responds to Burt's galvanizing presence in the room. He stands behind the keys. He karate chops the air, raises his chin and purses his lips. He emphasizes every dynamic shift by doing a deep knee bend at the piano.

Behind the glass, Phil is grinning, riding the faders. Hal is listening intently, eyes closed. Rocking to and fro, working the distance between her mouth and the Telefunken 251 mike, Dionne is pounding out the lyrics in the home stretch of a perfect take: 'I need your sweet love to ease, I need your sweet love to ease . . . all the pain.'

At two minutes forty-six seconds, the music stops. All eyes are on Burt. He looks at Dionne in the isolation booth and shakes his head in wonder, then back at Phil and Hal. He grins, 'Sensational, that killed me.' A bunch of string players spontaneously applauds.

Later, when the session wraps, there'll be time for a celebratory shot of Jack Daniel's at a nearby bar. But, for now, there are two more numbers to complete this afternoon.

Bacharach acted as producer, arranger, pianist and conductor, mostly out of what he has called 'self defence'. After those unhappy compromises in the early days, he insisted on complete control over his distinctively dramatic creations. His training in classical composition always inclined him towards imagining the music's big picture.

'When I was doing those songs with Dionne, I was thinking in terms of miniature movies, you know?' he says. 'Three-and-a-half minute movies with peak moments and not just one intensity level the whole way through. I never liked it where there's only one intensity from the singer, from the musical content, from the tracks and orchestration – it tends to beat you up.'

Even a partial list of Bacharach and David's three-and-a-half-minute movies is a staggering testament to the success of their vision: 'Anyone Who Had A Heart', 'I Just Don't Know What To Do With Myself', 'Here I Am', 'Wishin' And Hopin'', 'Are You There (With Another Girl)', 'You'll Never Get To Heaven (If You Break My Heart)', 'A House Is Not A Home', 'Message To Michael', 'Trains And Boats and Planes', 'The Windows Of The World', 'What The World Needs Now', '(There's) Always Something There To Remind Me', 'Do You Know The Way to San José', 'Paper

Maché', 'This Guy's In Love With You', 'I'll Never Fall In Love Again' and 'Raindrops Keep Fallin' On My Head.'

Throughout their peak years, the consistency of Bacharach and David's work never seemed to waver. Continuing to write in their lucky Brill Building cubicle as well as Burt's bachelor pad on East 61st Street in New York, the two hummed and clicked unstoppably. Burt delivered melody after glorious melody, each one full of unexpected pleasures and unforgettable hooks. His secret, then and now, is to write away from the piano.

'When you're sitting at the piano, you tend to go to what's familiar and you can get trapped by pretty chords,' Burt says. 'And you go by the step, by the beat.

'It's very hard for me to sit down and, as I'm writing at the piano, perceive this as a full song, knowing whether it's good or not good. It goes by in inches. If you get away from the piano and hear the melodic contour as well as the harmonization in your head, you're hearing a long vertical line. I like to take a long look at the song.

'I do that when I'm orchestrating too. I have a long-range picture of the whole scope of a piece. I get a sense of balance that I wouldn't get if I was sitting at the piano. Your hands tend to go places because they've been there before. You'll write what your hands can play instead of what an orchestration can play.'

Burt's orchestrations often included introductory phrases and instrumental breaks that were hooks in their own right – the flugelhorn on 'I'll Never Fall In Love Again', the marimba on 'Paper Maché'. 'When any instrumentalist would have a singular statement to make on a record, I'd write a lyric underneath,' he explains. 'It might be words that made no sense at all, but it would help them speak through their instruments. There are certain things that can't really be notated in orchestration. It's maybe two eighth notes, a sixteenth note and another eighth note, and that's the way it should be notated, but that's not the way it totally feels. But if you put words with it, or even vowel sounds, it does make a difference.'

Tailoring his lyrics to Bacharach's melodies, David also believed in taking a long, careful look. 'The first step is to listen to the music very closely, not so much to learn what the notes are, but to see what the music is saying to you. You should hear it talking to you. Sometimes the placement of the title was not so obvious with Burt's melodies. For instance, the chorus section in 'I Say A Little Prayer' – that's ordinarily where the title would fall, but it seemed to me that the title should come in the less obvious place, in the middle of the verse after "The moment I wake up, before I put on my make-up".

'Sometimes I'd write against the mood. For instance, 'Do You Know The Way To San José' is bright and rhythmic, and because of that you'd think

it was instinctively happy. But it wasn't to me.' With a sudden laugh, David half-apologizes, 'I do labour over these things. I spend inordinate amounts of time deciding whether "and" or "but" is the right word. To a certain extent, lyrics flow easily, but no matter how much they flow at a given time, by the time you get it together, finished and refined to the best of your ability, it's a lot of work.'

All this attention to their craft made Bacharach and David, by the late sixties, the most respected American songwriting team since Rogers & Hart. The offers and opportunities came pouring in. While Dionne maintained a steady chart presence, Burt and Hal lent their Midas touch to Sandie Shaw, Jack Jones, Aretha Franklin, Tony Bennett, Jackie DeShannon, Cher, Bobby Vinton, Brook Benton, Tom Jones, Cilla Black, Andy Williams, Herb Alpert, Sergio Mendes & Brasil '66, Barbra Streisand and many others. They scored films too: *Casino Royale* (in which Dusty Springfield cooed the definitive version of 'The Look Of Love') *The Man Who Shot Liberty Valance*, *Alfie*, *The Fool Killer*, *Send Me No Flowers*, *After the Fox*, *What's New Pussycat?*, *Wives and Lovers*, *Long Ago Tomorrow*, *April Fools* and the Academy Award-winning *Butch Cassidy and the Sundance Kid*. They also penned what was arguably the first rock opera, a 1965 TV special, *On The Flip Side*, which cast Ricky Nelson as a pop star whose career was on the slide.

Bacharach, with his sharply handsome looks, twinkling blue eyes, burnished fair hair and boyish charm, became a star in his own right, recording several solo albums of orchestrated instrumentals for A&M, now much sought after by the charity-store-browsing, cheesy-listening set that spawned the Mike Flowers Pops. Burt would occasionally sing on these compositions, in what liner notes then described as his 'earnest, rumpled baritone'. He also headlined sold-out concerts, appeared on TV variety shows and endorsed Martini in commercials.

In 1968, Burt and Hal, along with comic playwright Neil Simon, penned a Broadway musical, *Promises, Promises*, based on Billy Wilder's film *The Apartment*. Though it was extremely successful, earning a Tony Award and a lengthy run, it caused the first major ripple in the Bacharach-David partnership.

'Burt lost his enthusiasm for writing shows after that,' notes Hal. 'The experience was different than what he'd expected. He came out of a record-making background, where every time you play something it comes out the same. But in a show, there are so many variables: the tempo can be too fast, too slow, the singers can change lines or notes. If you're a perfectionist, it can drive you crazy.'

Bacharach, who caught pneumonia, fought physical exhaustion and says he was generally 'wiped out' during the process of mounting the show, comments, 'On some nights there might've been five or six subs in the orchestra. And my music is not easy to play. A song like "Promises, Promises" changes time signature in almost every bar.'

There were to be no further forays into theatre for the team. They closed out the final weeks of the sixties with their biggest hit yet, a simple folky tune complete with ukelele accompaniment, 'Raindrops Keep Falling On My Head.'

B. J. Thomas, who sang the Academy Award-winning smash, says he wasn't first in line for the vocal: 'Burt had orginally composed the melody to fit Bob Dylan. In subsequent years Burt has denied it, but this is what I understood at the time. Burt really admired Bob Dylan and the way he phrased. When Bob for whatever reasons didn't do it, I was his second choice. What's funny is that I actually had laryngitis and was barely able to eke out the thing for the soundtrack. But there's only maybe two or three times in my career when I felt like I'd recorded a hit record, no doubt, and that was one of them.'

'Raindrops' was also an example of Burt's increasing need for control over all aspects of record-making. 'I actually did stop it from coming out,' he recalled in 1980. 'It was set for release, but I turned down the pressing. I had been torn between two takes – one that sounded comfortable, one that had a lot of energy. I went with the comfortable. But what I wound up doing was making an edit right in the middle of the song, and picking up the fast one in the break. That's how it was finally released.'

Without breaking momentum, Burt and Hal greeted the seventies with a brace of potent dreamy-listening hits, including 'One Less Bell To Answer' by the Fifth Dimension and '(They Long To Be) Close To You' by the Carpenters. While neither seems to remember much about the writing of particular songs – David laughs, 'People always ask me what inspired such and such song and most times I'm not sure' – Hal does recall the source of 'One Less Bell To Answer'. 'Burt and I were in London working on a project, and I was invited to a dinner party. The hostess said to me, "When you arrive, don't ring the bell, just come in. It'll make one less bell for me to answer." I was wise enough to know it was a good title!'

As for 'Close To You' (which first appeared in 1964 as a B-side to Dionne's 'Here I Am') David admits, 'When Jerry Moss at A&M sent over the record of the Carpenters, I didn't think it was a hit. Not that Karen Carpenter didn't sound great – I just thought it didn't have what it took to really catch on. It shows that nobody, myself included, knows a hit until it becomes a hit.'

Despite a decade of continuous good fortune, trouble was brewing. While he was spending more time pursuing his own career with TV specials and

personal appearances, Bacharach's high profile marriage to actress Angie Dickinson ended. It's not hard to imagine that Burt's continuous presence in the limelight – their work started to be referred to as 'Burt Bacharach songs' – was by now irking his less flamboyant partner. When he and David got together in 1972 to compose songs for a musicalization of the Frank Capra film *Lost Horizon*, their chemistry faltered. The chunky soundtrack sung by a cast including Peter Finch, Liv Ullman and Charles Boyer, was roundly panned. *Newsweek* magazine called it 'excruciating'. From there, the reviews just got worse. Despite a heavy push, the dippity would-be hit from the movie, 'The World Is A Circle', failed to click with anyone.

By this time, apparently frazzled by the extremely negative response to their work, Burt and Hal were hardly on speaking terms. To compound the problems, lest she be sued by her record company, Dionne Warwick was forced to file a $6 million suit against the songwriters for failing to provide songs for her upcoming album. David then sued Bacharach over a publishing dispute (Hal refuses to talk about this now). Bacharach filed a countersuit.

They parted, and it wouldn't be until 1979 that the tangled suits were settled out of court. 'A part of me wanted to go all the way to court, but it wasn't a big enough part,' Bacharach commented in 1980. 'So I pushed to settle it because it was draining my energy. By moving to settle it I wound up paying considerably more than Mr David – he would have gone all the way to court.'

When the smoke cleared, Hal David eventually went on to collaborate with several different composers, turning out MOR smashes such as Ronnie Milsap's 'It Was Almost Like A Song' and the Willie Nelson–Julio Iglesias duet, 'To All The Girls I've Loved Before'. From 1980–86, he was president of ASCAP and continues to serve on the board of directors. The eldest of his two sons, Jim, manages Casa David, Hal's publishing company. 'Nowadays I'm writing songs with a few different people,' David reports. 'Pop songs with Archie Jordan and Kenny Hirsch, and theatre songs with Charles Strouse.' Somewhat wistfully Hal adds, 'Lyrics seem to be less important than thirty years ago. I wish I didn't think so. Very often the melodies seem less important. The sound and the production seem to be more important.'

After what he calls the 'giant bust' and a period of 'hiding out', Bacharach weathered the worst drought of his career. Between 1973 - 1981, he was absent from the charts while releasing two forgettable solo albums, *Woman* and *Futures*. Then in 1981 he married lyricist Carole Bayer Sager, and the two collaborated on a string of successful if somewhat schmaltzy hits: 'Arthur's Theme (The Moon And New York City)', 'Heartlight', 'On My Own' and 'That's What Friends Are For', a number one for Dionne Warwick and Friends. By the nineties, Burt had made a kind of peace with Hal and they got together once more at Dionne Warwick's request. Working at Burt's home in Del Mar, California, they attempted to rekindle the old magic. The result was one song, 'Sunny Weather Lover', a disappointingly flaccid track on Dionne's 1993 album *Friends Can Be Lovers*.

Currently, when he's not spending time with his family or indulging his passion for racehorses, Burt chooses his projects carefully. 'I still want to keep writing and have hits, but I find it very hard now, because it's just a different kind of scene. It's such a self-contained market. There are so many acts that write their own music and that's closing the doors a bit. I look for the opportunity to write a song for a specific purpose rather than saying, Let's see, what do we write today?, and me sitting down with John Bettis, writing a song then peddling it – I find that not so appealing at this time in my life.'

Curiously, this has prompted Burt to return to the dreaded stage. He's currently working on a modern musical retelling of *Snow White*, which he's writing with Mike And The Mechanics' lyricist and former solo artiste BA Robertson ('"The Living Years" is one of the finest lyrics in the ten years,' Burt declares). He has also collaborated with Elvis Costello on a new song, 'God Give Me Strength', for the upcoming motion picture *Grace of My Heart*.

'Elvis is terrific, a very good musician', he says. 'He had a musical input as well as lyrical. We never got together in person, we just did it over the phone, answering machines, fax machines and speaker phones. And it sounds great.'

Almost forty years after Bacharach and David first began shaking up the Brill Building, the tremors of their seismic influence can still be felt – it's Burt's picture prominently displayed in one corner of the cover of Oasis's *Definitely Maybe* and you can hear his influence in the syncopated trumpet break in Blur's 'The Universal'; it's there in artists as varied as Prefab Sprout, Luther Vandross, Elvis Costello, Pizzicato Five, Everything But The Girl, Jill Sobule and Gary Clark; it's there in the encomia from songwriters; it's there in lifts and shopping plazas courtesy of muzaky renditions of their songbook; but, most importantly, it's there in spirit every time an act breaks the rules and explores a new frontier in melodic pop music.

Of their far-searching and long-lasting legacy, David modestly concludes, 'When we were writing, Burt and I always tried to find something that was original. There was no fun in being like everyone else.'

(First published in *Mojo*, 1996.)

classic

Burt Bacharach

'Pacific Coast Highway' (3.20)
Album: On The Move (Chevrolet) 1970
A deceptively powerful and sophisticated arrangement which more than warrants its title – putting one in mind of swaying palms, the cool Californian breeze and open-top sports cars hurtling through Santa Monica. So successful was this tune that it was used to advertise the 1970 range of Chevrolet cars, including the Caprice, the Monte Carlo and the Chevelle SS 396.

classic

Burt Bacharach

'Wives & Lovers' (2.46)
Album: Hit Maker! (Kapp) 1965
As easycore instrumentals go, they don't get much better than this, the definitive recording of the first commercially successful jazz waltz.

John Barry
by David Toop

York in the late thirties. Sibelius fills the room. The heroic clamour of his first symphony. Maurice Ravel's fluttering, sunlit 'Daphnis et Chloé' or Stravinsky's 'The Rite Of Spring' hurtling round the turntable of the Prendergast family gramophone at seventy-eight revolutions per minute. The young John Barry Prendergast deploys his Dinky toys and his metal soldiers into warfare or car crashes.

London in the middle eighties. John Barry takes it easy with a Scotch after a day on the adult toys, the grand piano and the Moviola. 'Some people ride bicycles,' he says. 'I used to sit there with Dinky toys and play classical music. It was part of my dramatic narrative as a child. It was very much done in private. If anybody walked into the room . . .'

John Barry. *The* James Bond soundtrack composer, cult figure, arranger, Grammy winner, four Oscars, filmscores for *Jagged Edge, The Cotton Club, Peggy Sue Got Married, Out of Africa, Howard the Duck,* and, going backwards, *Hammett, Body Heat, The Day of the Locust, Monte Walsh, Midnight Cowboy, The Lion in Winter, Dutchman, Born Free, The Knack . . . and How to Get It, The Ipcress File, Seance on a Wet*

In his time John Barry has conquered just about every musical form, from rock'n'roll, pop and swingbeat to orchestral arrangements, movie scores and even classical recordings. During the last forty years he has proved to be one of the most influential conductors of all time

Afternoon, *Zulu*, *Beat Girl*. Add another sixty or more scores to that. A number one with Duran Duran and 'A View To A Kill' in 1985. Collaborations with A-Ha and Chrissie Hynde on the new Bond, *The Living Daylights.*

Impressive.

When I first talked to Barry he was just completing work on *A View to a Kill.* As a New York resident, the only indications he had to his cult status in Britain came from pop stars – Paul Young looking for some production, or John Taylor, who Barry says, knows more about stuff that I've done than I know myself. He'd pick out a scene from an old movie and talk about it like I'm supposed to remember it.'

Perhaps his career began there on the living-room carpet, orchestrating the action with classical music. 'I think I'm one of the few people who started off wanting to be a movie composer,' he says. 'I think you'll find most movie composers drifted into it in a strange way. They were arrangers or this, that and the other. Because my father had eight cinemas and because I was brought up from four years old on Mickey Mouse or whatever, it was something I very positively wanted to do. By the time I was sixteen, seventeen years old I'd probably seen more films than anybody else because of my circumstances. That was in York. My father had two theatres in York, one in Hull, one in Scarborough, various other places. I mean, at fourteen years old I could run the whole projection box. If the projectionist was ill I could go up there and do it.'

John Barry studied piano at St. Peter's School in York, a public school which discouraged any aspirations towards a musical career. This being the era of national service, he then joined the army. 'Three years I served Her Majesty,' he says, with no trace of an American accent and not much Yorkshire either. 'I was in a military band playing trumpet, cornet, whatever. When I came out I started doing some arrangements and it was going nowhere fast. The whole popular music thing was starting and I thought, well, Christ, this seems like a way to get started. I had a few friends who'd been in the army with me and a few friends who'd been in a dance band in Scarborough so we put a group together and totally imitated what was going on at that time – Bill Haley, Freddie Bell and the Bellboys.

'We bought the first bass guitar in England, a German thing called a Hofner. We were the first group to have a bass guitar and a couple of amplifiers. When I look at what goes out there now, you know . . . one million dollars worth of equipment. I mean, we had £35 amplifiers, two of them, and we thought we were really hot shit.

'It was just a means of getting ahead quicker. When you're young you don't want to stick around. The big bands were falling apart. Jack Parnell was having trouble keeping a sixteen piece band going and I had a band that made ten times more noise than his.' He laughs wickedly. 'That was it. That was the turnaround.'

The mood of the times in the adult dominated music industry was that rock'n'roll was a passing phase. Fads like calypso came and went and the dominant wish was that the big bands would soon return. During his spell in the army, Barry had spent his service pay on a correspondence course with American West Coast arranger Bill Russo, famous for his work with the Stan Kenton Orchestra. His ability to read and write music, play an instrument and arrange, made it easy for him to create a legitimate backdrop for the newly emerging British pop stars. The John Barry Seven auditioned with agent Harold Feilding and began an immediate season with Tommy Steele at the Palace, Blackpool, backing the entire show and playing their own spot. 'I hated performing,' he says. 'Going out on stage was the dread of my life. I got out of it as soon as I could.' He provided music for the TV pop shows of the late fifties and early sixties, *Drumbeat*, *Oh Boy* and the theme for *Juke Box Jury*. Archive footage of the BBC's *Six-Five Special*, circa 1958, reveals a slightly uncomfortable and artistically feeble stab at a vocal career. Like many musicians before or since, Barry was in search of a pop idol to front the stage.

By the end of 1959 he had a number one single with Adam Faith singing 'What Do You Want'. The singing style was Buddy Holly via vulnerable cockney sparrer (a persona later to come to its full flowering in *Budgie*). The music was known as stringbeat. It was Barry's reworking of American pop: the twangy guitar sound of Duane Eddy mixed with a light backbeat and distinctive pizzicato violins inspired by Dick Jacobs's string arrangement on Buddy Holly's 'It Doesn't Matter Anymore'.

Adam Faith's hits gave Barry the opportunity he needed. 'I'd been a musical director at EMI Records,' he says, 'and I'd had a lot of success with Adam Faith. Adam was asked to star in a movie called *Beat Girl* which was a youth movie of that period and so I was asked to do the score. It was a pretty horrendous kind of movie of the time – supposedly the beat generation.' Certainly, some of the period-flavour dialogue is laughably off-target – 'Say baby, you feel Terpsichorical?' – but the soundtrack shows that Barry's real strength lay not in playing slight pop tunes but in creating atmosphere and impact for celluloid images. *Beat Girl* was the first British film soundtrack to be released on record. Its re-issue in 1985 made comparisons with *Absolute Beginners* inevitable. The vote, it must be said, goes heavily in favour of *Beat Girl*.

What follows is something of a mystery. The first James Bond film, *Dr. No*, was scored by Monty Norman. It is a largely undistinguished soundtrack with the exception of the James Bond theme, credited to Norman but played on record by the John Barry Seven. Barry's arrangement is simply

one of the best instrumental records ever made. Sexual, suave, dramatic, haunting and perfectly paced. Timeless.

I've read that you wrote that tune, not Monty Norman, I say. Is that true? There's a long pause. 'That's the difficult question of all time,' he finally answers. 'I'll ask you a question. If Monty Norman wrote it, why isn't he still scoring the rest of the movies?' Anybody looking for clues should listen to a Barry composition called 'Black Stockings' which spent nine weeks in the charts in 1960. The fade-out is strongly reminiscent of the James Bond theme intro. 'Black Stockings' predates the 'James Bond Theme' by two years.

What is it like to work on Bond soundtracks? I ask. 'It's the longest job I ever had,' he says. 'It's the most successful series of films ever made. It's a very successful formula. You know that when it opens it's going to have a huge audience. That's almost unique in the film industry. No one can conceive of it being a failure, which is very strange.'

Which is your favourite Bond score? 'It has to be *Goldfinger*,' he says. 'It was a question of finding the style. *From Russia With Love* consolidated after *Dr. No*. I'm not just talking from a musical point of view. I'm talking about directional and stylistic point of view. *Goldfinger* came together. They knew what they'd got. It had a freshness and an energy. It was the true birth. That was the style and everybody felt secure in it. Also, it had the edge to it. And then, after that, without being disrespectful, it was formula time. It was a good formula, like grand Mickey Mouse opera. Very high style.

'"Goldfinger" was the craziest song ever. Weird song. We couldn't have written that song *as* a song. I remember I went to Tony Newley to write the lyric. He said, "What the hell do I do with it?" I said, It's *"Mack The Knife."* It just worked. Robert Brownjohn's extraordinary visuals for the titles . . . Shirley Bassey didn't know what the song was about but she sang it with such extraordinary conviction that she convinced the rest of the world that it meant something. Shirley hates performing that now. She *hates* it. It's a very awful song to perform. She says, 'I've gotta do that song everywhere, John, you bastard.' It's the bane of her life. It was funny when she did Carnegie Hall. The orchestra went baaah baaah,' and here he imitates the opening cords of 'Goldfinger', 'and the whole audience stood up and went waaaah! It's awful to do that to somebody.

'I remember I read in an interview in *Films and Filming* once. Somebody asked Fellini what his favourite score was and he said *Goldfinger*. The guy didn't ask Fellini anything else – he was in such a state of shock. He obviously expected some hugely intellectual work so he didn't even ask him how or why or what. That was the end of the interview. I bumped into Fellini in a lift – the elevator in the Plaza hotel in New York. He didn't know me. He had no reason to. As we were going up in the lift I said. 'Excuse me, somebody said your favourite film score is *Goldfinger*. I'm John Barry.' He said, "Oh yes!", shook hands and walked straight out of the lift.'

Barry has worked with many different lyricists on the Bond title songs. One of them, Hal David, is perhaps best-known for his work with Burt Bacharach on songs like 'Walk On By', 'Anyone Who Had A Heart' and 'I Say A Little Prayer'. 'One of my favourite Bond songs,' says Barry, 'the least successful, is "We Have All The Time In the World". I love that song and it's Hal David's favourite song, funnily enough. The pleasure of it was working with Louis Armstrong. He was very ill but when he sang 'wuh-yuld' we all just broke up. I'm very emotionally attached to that song and that whole thing with Armstrong. It was the last record he made.

'How can you tell about hits? That died the death. Nobody wanted to know. Then, three years later the same record went to number one in Italy, number one for nine months! I go to Italy and it's "Hey-a, Mr. Barry. You wrote 'All The Time In The World'. It's-a lovely song." It was one disc jockey who for some obscure reason – maybe he was drunk one night – started to play it on this Rome radio station and it went like a . . .'

Over one year later and we are lunching in Wheeler's in Old Compton Street. The rain is pouring down. Don't you just miss all this? I ask. Barry has just been the lucky prizewinner of a Fleet Street *Tax Exile Ex-Husband of Sex Kitten Jane Birkin James Bond Composer Slams Britain* type profile in the *Daily Mail*. The real reason for talking to the *Mail* was to discuss the Oscar for *Out of Africa*, the number one with Duran Duran or the highly acclaimed score for *Jagged Edge*, one of the best films of 1986. Where's the scandal in that?

By that point Barry had made up with Francis Ford Coppola after the agonies of *Cotton Club* and written the score for *Peggy Sue Got Married*. 'I told Francis this is taking me back to my roots,' said Barry, amused to be recreating Buddy Holly music once more. He was also reflecting on the new possibilities of electronics after working with Duran Duran and Bernard Edwards in New York's Power Station and using synthesizers instead of an orchestra for *Jagged Edge*.

Into each life a little rain must fall, as the song goes. Another year goes by. What have you been up to? I ask. 'I did *Howard the Duck* for my sins,' he says. 'They gave me a last-minute call to do it and I thought it would be exciting to work with George Lucas. As it was, I never saw George Lucas once and nobody went to see the goddam movie.' He also worked on *Goldenchild*. After disastrous previews, forty minutes of footage were cut from the film in two weeks and Barry was asked to rescore. He declined. 'It's been a long hot summer,' he says.

Now he's in and out of the studio with Chrissie Hynde, finishing up her songs for *The Living Daylights*. She sings 'Where Has Everybody Gone?',

a song that concerns a villain who strangles people with Walkman headphones, and the end title theme, 'Where Have I Seen You?' Working with A-Ha, he describes as being like 'playing ping pong with four balls.'

'Everybody does bad scores,' he said two years ago, sitting next to the grand piano and the Moviola. 'We've all got dogs in our closet but we work. People think we sit around until *Gone with the Wind* or *Citizen Kane* is offered to us but we function. That's how we earn our living. Every filmscore isn't a dream. There's a reality to it. 'The most important thing for movie writing is the atmosphere, the spirit, the uplift. Being accurate to a scene – hitting that scene's feelings accurately and giving it the sense of tragedy, joy, whatever it is. That's the fun of it. I adore music but when I'm sitting there watching that,' and he nods at the Moviola by the fireplace, 'that's the boss. The picture is God. Music is secondary.'
(First published in *The Face*, 1987.)

classic

John Barry

'Into Vienna' (2.44)
Album: The Living Daylights (Warner Brothers) 1987
The great forgotten Bond movie, the great forgotten Bond soundtrack. This is a delicious Barry instrumental which is also included on the LP as 'If There Was A Man' by the Pretenders. The other great forgotten Bond soundtrack is *Never Say Never Again,* and in particular Lani Hall's theme tune (which, incidentally, only includes one chorus).

classic

John Barry

'The Girl With The Sun In Her Hair' (2.50)
Album: The Persuaders! (CBS) 1971
This tune, written for a shampoo ad, is swamped in strings, showing that even Barry's less austere work was head and shoulders above the rest.

Les Baxter

The archetypal virtual tourist, this Texan composer offered baby-boomer suburbanites the chance to explore hitherto taboo regions of illicit sex and exotic ritual, 'a sonic conjurer of vicarious experience,' according to David Toop, author of *Ocean of Sound*. Originally a saxophonist who performed in Californian clubs in the forties, he went on to work as an arranger and musical director for Mel Tormé, Nat 'King' Cole, Bob Hope and Abbot & Costello. In 1953 he scored his first movie, a sailboat travelogue called *Tanga Tika,* and never looked back, over the last thirty-five years creating soundtracks for dozens and dozens of films, including *The Raven, House of Usher, The Man With X-Ray Eyes, Beach Blanket Bingo, How to Stuff a Wild Bikini* and *Wild in the Streets*. It was his own, highly personal work which made him notable, however, along with Martin Denny and Arthur Lyman inventing the hyper-world of exotica.

Joseph Lanza notes that Baxter, along with his fellow exoticists, represented 'a celebration of America's power to mould the unknown in the image of reconstructed psychosexual fantasies of GIs who had been stationed in the islands during World War II'. Baxter excelled at space-age bachelor pad music, creating enchanting little symphonies which conjured up exotic images of the Gold Coast, the South Pacific, the Andes, even other planets. 'What I like about Baxter is his overkill orchestration in the fine tradition of Carl Orff, Busby Berkeley and Magma,' says former Dead Kennedy Jello Biafra in *Incredibly Strange Music Volume II* (Re/Search 1994). 'A quiet five-piece cocktail number by [Martin] Denny will, in Baxter's hands, becomes a full orchestra with

dozens of deep baritone voices singing *ooh* and *aah* choruses to create the mood of the jungle. If Les Baxter decides to do a folk album, he won't use one person with a guitar – no, he'll use eight guitars and a banjo player *plus* his orchestra! Move over, Kingston Trio – here comes the whole Kingston family!' Towards the end of Baxter's career, the soundtrack business dried up, so he wrote a considerable amount of music for theme parks and seaworlds, as David Toop suggests, 'surely the ultimate PoMo job'. He died in 1996, aged seventy-three.

'I write difficult music,' Les Baxter once declared proudly. 'You know Stravinsky's "Petrouchka"? I don't know of any scores as concert-like and as advanced as my scores. My scores were "Petrouchka" – Stravinsky, Ravel. Other people's scores were movie music'

The Beach Boys

While it is true that Brian Wilson invented California, he has never been fully able to enjoy his spoils; trapped, seemingly, in an internal – and eternal – world of foreboding, panic and insecurity. The only thing which has saved him from true madness is his awesome talent for sweet music.

Like Bacharach, Brian Wilson had the ability to mix euphoria and melancholia in the space of a single song, often the same melody, and occasionally the same note. Given his huge personal problems (an aggressive and belligerent father, a dysfunctional family, a fragile mental state, weight problems and a long-standing over-bearing therapist), it's hardly surprising that Wilson's best music always had an innate sadness, a tender quality which can be found in such diverse Beach Boy songs as 'Our Prayer', 'Wind Chimes', 'The Lonely Sea', 'Caroline No', 'Surf's Up', 'The Warmth Of The Sun' (written in response to the Kennedy assassination) and his greatest triumph, 'Till I Die' (a version of which appears on their 1971 LP *Surf's Up*, though the vastly superior instrumental has long been available on bootleg). As Nick Kent has so eloquently written, Wilson wrote 'harmonies so complex, so graceful they

Brian Wilson's reaction to living in a world without love was to write and inspire some of the loveliest songs ever recorded: 'In My Room', 'Don't Worry Baby', 'Please Let Me Wonder', 'You're So Good To Me', 'And Your Dreams Come True', 'Surf's Up', 'The Warmth Of The Sun' and nearly a hundred more

seemed to have more in common with a Catholic Mass than any cocktail-lounge accapella doo-wop.'

The Beach Boys myth, however, is an enduring one, even though it has been disproved time and time again. And while any history of the group must now include sibling rivalry, domestic violence, appalling drug abuse, death, madness, and internecine lawsuits, the popular images of bronzed beach babes, hot-rods, and roller-skating carhops at the Wilshire Boulevard Dolores Drive-In have become as iconic as those grainy black and white photographs of the Beatles rushing through the streets of London pursued by hundreds of screaming schoolgirls; none of it was particularly true, though now it's too late to deny.

The songs, though, are as true as anything cast in vinyl: everything from 'Surfin' USA', 'California Girls' and 'Spirit Of America' to 'Fun Fun Fun', 'God Only Knows' and 'I Get Around' epitomizing all that was once white and willing about American youth.

Brian Wilson's more obvious influences have been well documented (the Four Freshmen, Phil Spector, mid-period Beatles), though a lot of his orchestration and arrangements owe much to Martin Denny and Les Baxter (and in particular tracks such as 'Miserlou' and 'Voodoo Dreams/Voodoo') as well as other exponents of exotica, like Yma Sumac (Amy Camus) and Tak Shindo. Even Wilson's most innocent and naive melodies have a hint of pathos about them, and using exotica's bizarre array of references (eerie choral repetition, jungle noises – 'Pet Sounds' – staccato keyboards), he found himself able to conjure up the most sublime parables of hope and desperation (*Pet Sounds,* in the words of journalist Peter Doggett, 'conjures up the volatile ecstasy and despair of teenage romance within a context of loss, love and self-awareness that can only come from the experience of adulthood'); music which seemed like it had spent a thousand years 20,000 leagues beneath the surf.

Recently the ageing Beach Boy's official releases have tended to sound unnervingly like nursery rhymes (particularly some of the more arcane material on *Orange Crate Art,* his Van Dyke Parks collaboration), and his legacy is in the hands of people like the High Llamas, who have given themselves a remit to finish the album that Wilson never could, *Smile.* There is always the chance , however, that the tortured genius will – almost in spite of himself – inadvertently throw in some descending minor chord which – perhaps helped by cascading strings, soaring horns and the fat twang of a cheap guitar – finds itself imbued with the power to break hearts from California to Beijing.

'I'm getting there,' he says, from the one side of his face which still seems to want to talk to the world. 'I'm forcing my way out. It's almost as though I went into an egg and just had to poke my way out of it.'

Brian Wilson, like a cork on the ocean . . .

For much of the seventies, Brian Wilson was in a world of his own: 'I was a useless little vegetable. I made everybody very angry at me because I wasn't able to work, to get off my butt. Coke every day. Goin' over to parties. Just having bags of snow around, snortin' it down like crazy'

The Brill Building was the home of the ampersand, the place where many songwriting partnerships first gelled. Many have tried to emulate the Brill's fantastic success, yet it was a product of time, circumstance and, to a certain extent, naiveté. Alas, all things must pass

classic

Beach Boys
'Our Prayer' (1.06)
Album: 20/20 (Capital) 1969
Originally recorded in 1966 for *Smile,* this is a wordless rhapsody, what Brian Wilson called 'rock church music'. Rothko, eat your heart out.

classic

Beach Boys
'The Nearest Faraway Place' (2.36)
Album: 20/20 (Capital) 1969
Composed, performed and produced by Bruce Johnson, this shows the Brothers Beach at their most whimsical, recorded during a period when they were largely ignored (both by critics and the public). The strings here are arranged by the future disco baron, Van McCoy. 'Bruce did a very beautiful thing with [this],' said Brian Wilson.

classic

Bjork
'Come To Me' (4.55)
Album: Debut (One Little Indian) 1993
Captain Scarlet in the slumber lounge. A haunting love song arranged by trendier-than-thou producer Nellee Hooper, a beautiful if slightly disconcerting ballad that perhaps wouldn't have existed had it not been for Martin Denny and Gerry Anderson. Is Captain Black in the house?

The Brill Building
Located at the corner of Broadway and 49th Street, the Brill Building was, during the fifties and early sixties, the Pentagon of Pop, 'Teen Pan Alley', an eleven-storey address which housed every jobbing songwriter on the block, including Leiber & Stoller, Barry & Greenwich, and Goffin & King. In dark and invariably smoke-filled cubbyholes, with perhaps only a piano, a bench and maybe a chair for the lyricist, hundreds of young and established songwriters would bash away at their three-minute masterpieces, and then try and place them with the dozens of publishing companies which occupied the rest of the building. Once the home of the great American standard, after the emergence of rock'n'roll the Brill Building became the breeding ground of every aspiring Phil Spector, with baby-faced songwriters falling over themselves to pen the latest hit for the Shirelles or the Drifters. 'Two of its most gifted graduates were Burt

Bacharach and Hal David,' writes Paul Du Noyer, 'who escaped the teenage ghetto via sophisticated songs of adult romance. Like the Brill itself, they were a link to the older world of American popular song. And perhaps the wordsmith, Hal David, gets overlooked: his scenarios ("Trains And Boats And Planes", "24 Hours From Tulsa", "Do You Know The Way To San José" etc.) were vivid and essential. Years earlier, when somebody remarked that Jerome Kern had written "Ol' Man River", the wife of Kern's lyricist Oscar Hammerstein interrupted sharply. "Indeed not," she scolded. "Jerome Kern wrote 'dum dum dum-dum.' My husband wrote 'Ol' Man River'." '

classic

The Dave Brubeck Quartet
'Take 5' (5.23)
Album: Time Out (CBS) 1959
It's jazz, but then it's not jazz, not really. Written by Brubeck's alto saxophonist Paul Desmond, this has often been derided as rather a white, middle-class buttoned-down example of 'airline' jazz, yet it has become an iconic formalist classic as well as the perfect cocktail party accessory. The Quartet's 'Blue Rondo A La Turk', with its Mozart echoes, is another tune in the same vein from the same LP.

During the early sixties it was difficult to find an American home without a copy of Brubeck's *Time Out* LP (like *Saturday Night Fever, Rumours* and *Frampton Comes Alive!* after it), while the music itself has become so familiar that no one actually hears what's going on any more

Easy Discs

Dig the mariachi man! Brimming with corn-fed rude health, Herb Alpert turned his dreams into music, and his music into money, aided by one astonishingly good idea and his trusty magic trumpet

He might have been born way down in Kansas City, yet Burt Bacharach was New York through and through, a living embodiment of urban, urbane cool, the hippest pianist in the world. Ever

Often maligned as a conjuror of the fanciful and the flighty, Bacharach's middle name was complexity. 'Anyone Who Had A Heart', for instance, deftly weaves through 5/4, 4/4 and 7/8

Few of us carry on without a soundtrack running parallel to our lives; few of us have soundtracks which don't include something from the Tsar of orchestral arrangement, the great, *great* John Barry

Easy Discs

Persuaded? This 1971 action-comedy series was at least a decade ahead of its time, while Barry's haunting theme remains fastened to the period like the broken zipper on a pair of purple slacks

'I got a little exotic there for a while,' Baxter would say. 'People said, "Where did it come from, that sound, did you go to Brazil? Cuba? Africa?" At the time I never got further than Glendale'

The ad said it all: 'It's Brian, Dennis, Carl, Al and Mike's greatest ever! Contains their all-time best-selling single . . . AND . . . an exciting full-color sketchbook look inside the world of Brian Wilson'

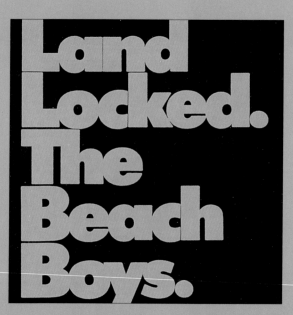

The second great lost Beach Boys album, containing intricate versions of 'Take A Load Off Your Feet', 'Big Sur', 'Lookin' At Tomorrow' and, of course, the monumental 'Till I Die', a solid gold classic

Easy Discs

Tony Bennett was among many singers who traded in their torch songs for lifestyle ballads as soon as it became expedient to do so. He released this particular collection of same in 1995

Talkin' Loud's 1994 Brazilian pot-pourri is an essential compilation featuring Sergio Mendes, Jorge Ben, Edu Lobo, Baden Powell, Milton Nascimento, the Tamba Trio and more. Virtually seamless

The first post-punk group to totally embrace the hi-fi, space-age iconography of suburban America during the late fifties and early sixites, the B-52's were convertible and cruisin'

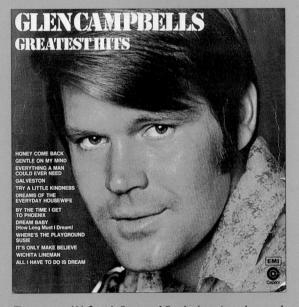

The crossover kid, Campbell successfully mixed country and pop, and with the help of Jimmy Webb – 'Wichita Lineman' (1968), 'Galveston' (1969) etc – recorded a series of intriguingly wistful ballads

Easy Discs

It simply must be him. 'I wasn't the first to use voices as instruments,' says Ray Conniff. 'But I was the first to put voices right alongside instruments until you couldn't tell them apart'

The space-age bachelor pad has become an enduring and durable image, used to market everything from credit cards and designer suits to sports cars and beer. This sleeve dates from 1966

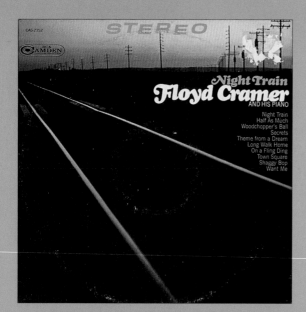

Having played piano on Elvis's 'Heatbreak Hotel', Floyd Cramer developed a unique playing style that gave his instrument a slat-key twang, a 'countrypolitan' sound that made his keys shimmer

As suburban as a Tupperware party, Ray Davies's Button-Down Brass took contemporary family pop and turned it into a cascade of trumpet-fuelled kitsch. A truly remarkable group

Easy Discs

Having helped Hawaii develop into a mythical island paradise by performing at Honolulu's Hawaiian Village nightclub, Denny became as much of a tourist attraction as Pearl Harbor or Diamond Head

The Mexican maestro stripped lyrics from pop standards and replaced them with whistling, humming, disjointed phrases and his by-now-famous refrain, 'Zu-zu-zu'. And he meant it

When Fifth Dimension members Marilyn McCoo and Billy Davis got married, the ceremony was performed in a hot-air balloon as a nod towards Jimmy Webb, and 'Up, Up & Away'

After-dark retro practitioners, the Gentle People deliberately evoke a future made possible by a world full of highballs, jet travel, two-car garages and appliance-filled fitted kitchens

Easy Discs

Stan Getz played many things with many people. However, it was the bossa-nova that gave him his big commercial break, and is the thing for which he is best remembered

Crying all over the world. The ultimate in feminine sounds, Astrud Gilberto's voice was more evocative than anyone at first thought. It was a popular noise, too, an evergreen one

Morton Gould was a champion of 'light' music decades before it became fashionable, using his considerable talents to experiment with light salon arrangements, supper tunes and 'slumber music'

Herbie Hancock's pitch-perfect soundtrack to Antonioni's fetishistic period-piece *Blow-Up* (made in 1966, starring David Hemmings, Sarah Miles and Jane Birkin) is a fair approximation of Swinging London

Easy Discs

What Astrud Gilberto was to Brazil, so Françoise Hardy was to France. A heart-breaker to look at, apparently all she could sing about was broken hearts. It hardly makes one love her less

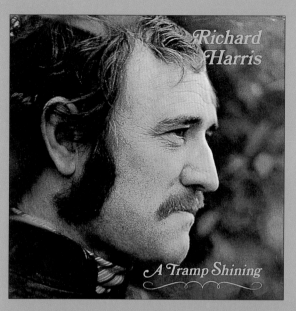

A man called hoarse? Unlike the kitsch exercises by William Shatner and Dirk Bogarde, Richard Harris's albums (initiated by Jimmy Webb) proved that he could sing as well as act (just)

If he had perhaps applied himself, Tony Hatch could have been the British Bacharach, but he was always rather generous with his talents, and succumbed a lot to television

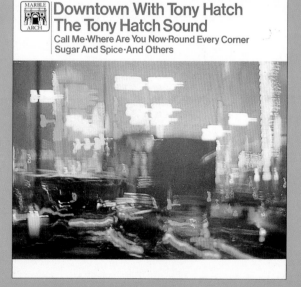

Hatch appeared to write songs as casually as shopping lists, though they were great lists: 'Man Alive', 'Where Are You Now', 'Don't Sleep In The Subway', 'Downtown', 'The Champions' etc

Easy Discs

Black Moses, The Buddha of the Ballad, Blacharach. Isaac Hayes has been called many things, not least a masterful orchestral arranger, a waterbed crooner and Shaft's super-fine alter-ego (1971)

Easy does it. When it comes to singing telegrams, there were few crooners to compare with Michael Holliday, a man for whom the microphone might have been invented

Jimmy Webb gave this Mississippi-born, California-raised singer her breakthrough with this record, released in 1969, describing Houston's talents as 'everything great about the black female voice'

Frank Sinatra once referred to Jack Jones as his natural successor, and while his career hasn't quite equalled that of his mentor, certain songs remain his, and his alone (1964)

classic

The B-52's

'Follow Your Bliss' (4.10)

Album: Cosmic Thing (Reprise) 1989

Recorded for their comeback LP by Nile Rodgers, this futuristic and seriously funky guitar-based instrumental is as good as any sixties surf single – summertime incarnate, with no strings attached.

Left: Glen Campbell: 'Gentle On My Mind', 'Wichita Lineman', 'Rhinestone Cowboy', 'Southern Nights', 'Turn Around Look At Me', 'By The Time I Get To Phoenix', 'Galveston', 'Where's The Playground Susie', 'All I Have To Do Is Dream', 'Dream Baby', 'Let It Be Me'

Above: Formed in 1976, towards the end of the decade the B-52's were lauded from Georgia to Georgetown for their arty trash aesthetic, while their underwater dance party classic 'Rock Lobster' became a campus favourite. Hairstyle or bomber, who cared?

classic

Glen Campbell

'Wichita Lineman' (2.59)

Single (Capitol) 1968

That nomadic bassline, those sexy strings . . . Campbell's majestic version of Jimmy Webb's road song – along with Nilsson's version of 'Everybody's Talkin' from the same period – has always evoked some kind of existential euphoria. Webb and Campbell collaborated on many occasions ('By The Time I Get To Phoenix', 'Galveston', 'Where's The Playground Susie', 'Honey Come Back'), but nothing ever touched this. Few things ever have.

'We are a pop group, that's all,' say the Cardigans with typical self-deprecation. 'We aim to please.' Pure pop has become such a pejorative term that you wonder why people still try and excel at it. Yet they do, in ever-increasing numbers. The Cardigans, for their sins, concede nothing but affection for the past

Right: Calling occupants of interplanetary bri-nylon leisure suits. Richard and Karen Carpenter were the epitome of shrink-wrapped, white-bread America, producing songs full of intimate and densely layered harmonies, delicate piano lines and sympathetic string arrangements

The Cardigans

Rather unfairly referred to as the Swedish Pizzicato Five, or else the true heirs to the Abba legacy, this co-ed Stockholm quartet are actually the finest exponents of lounge pop in all Scandinavia. Their almost-remarkable album *Life* (Minty Fresh Records, 1995) contains thirteen original songs (including 'Daddy's Car', which is begging to be covered by Dionne Warwick) as well as a bizarre and not totally successful version of Black Sabbath's 'Sabbath Bloody Sabbath'.

The Carpenters
by Kodwo Eshun

Abhorred in the seventies, a cult in the eighties, revered in the nineties: the fall and rise and rise of the Carpenters should be written as a question – how did a duo reviled for selling nearly a hundred million records worldwide become fêted by nineties alternative rock? *If I Were A Carpenter*, the tribute album which commemorates twenty-five years of the Carpenters, takes in the college rock of American Music Club and Red Kross, the singer/songwriters Matthew Sweet and Grant Lee Buffalo, and the all-girl groups Babes In Toyland and Shonen Knife. All treat the Carpenters with a seriousness that would have shocked them, a hushed intensity more like Woodstock than the Ed Sullivan show.

On a good day in 1970, the Carpenters' music could turn the mildest of Aquarians into an Ayatollah in denim, the most bovine of hippies into a snarling punk. On a bad day, when their Dentyne-bright harmonies rang out like the bell on the gates of white heaven, Karen and Richard Carpenter sounded like cheerleaders for the HUAC. 'Young Americans at their best,' Nixon called them when he invited the duo to sing round at his place in September 1973. Watergate was about to break, Vietnam was required nightly viewing, conspiracy movies such as *The Parallax View* and *The Conversation* were peaking and there was Karen singing about a jilted groupie listening to the radio for Tricky Dickie and Willy Brandt. At a point when the FBI were keeping tabs on rock stars, the Carpenters, like James Brown, were moderate Republicans.

Their pristine halos of sound seeped through the fabric of the seventies, into its travel agencies and airport lobbies, hotel foyers and office elevators, like an updated version of Huxley's *Soma*. They sold millions of albums, lured American youth away from the fun of Nam and the thrill of

Black Power, away from Hendrix and Cream, back into the serene sleep of perfect pop. That was the standard *Rolling Stone* line of the time. To an audience who could see the stage sets behind Neil Armstrong, who wondered why the Apollo transmissions sounded so close (as if they came not from the moon but . . . Montana!)

The Carpenters' ubiquity had to be a propaganda job, a government set-up. If you were attuned to media disinformation, and everyone was in the seventies, the strategy was transparent. In the fifties, Cold War prosperity encouraged exotica, the music of Les Baxter and films such as *South Pacific*, which remade the world as a fantasy playground for the US. In the seventies, with crack-ups converging faster than anyone could count, the new zeitgeist was Domestica. Invent some soft sitcoms such as *The Brady Bunch* and *The Partridge Family*, invest in some cute groups such as the Osmonds and the Carpenters and damp down the situation. Dumbing everything down: that was the verdict from friends and enemies alike.

Until 1983, that is, when Karen died from heart failure at the age of thirty-two, the first star to die from what the chat shows were calling the 'slimming disease'. For this audience, anorexia transformed Karen Carpenter from a tremulous, sexless waif before the Waif, into pop's Sylvia Plath. 'Close To You' and 'We've Only Just Begun', 'Superstar' and 'Goodbye To Love' – the surface gleam and orchestral sweep of these songs was smelted down into tragic metal, until they sounded unbearably melancholic and yet strangely detached, excerpts from one woman's war of attrition, snatches of a seven-year locked groove of obsessive unhappiness. Richard's Qualude addiction, his only redeeming vice, only added to their rising shares on the Rock Death Index.

Everything the hippies thought about them turned out to be wrong. They had figured the siblings as Ken and Barbie come to life. Richard, they recalled, always looked as if he'd bartered his balls for dentures. And hadn't Karen's outfits inspired the Stepford Wives? *People* magazine's front cover story and the endless profiles which followed Karen's death revealed a hidden life that utterly contradicted the public one. Karen's anorexia was the fall-out from nuclear normality, the result of dysfunction beneath the family romance. As Ray Coleman writes in *The Carpenters: the Untold Story*, Karen, Richard and their mother Agnes were locked into a vicious loop of dependency. Agnes would veto Karen's boyfriends. Karen would drive away Richard's girlfriends. Richard, torn between these demands, would cave into the family. Even when they finally left home in their mid-twenties, they shared a house – Karen with her collection of toy animals and Richard alone.

'America's most defiant squares,' *The New York Times* snickered in

1991. The effort needed to sustain that squareness is what fascinates the eighties and nineties indie generations. Johnny Cash, Andy Williams, Johnny Carson, Carole Burnett, Ed Sullivan and Perry Como – Karen and Richard plugged into the light entertainment circuit as if rock wasn't big enough. They radiated health and an obsessive ordinariness that blossomed under ABC studio lights. It's as if all that beaming made them ill. Anorexia's utter self-consciousness made it the perfect media illness, a kind of image sickness that was more talked about than understood. Watching them now, Richard with his gangling frame, his hair, chipper and cheerful, his smile, effortlessly shit-eating, and Karen with her eerie Ali McGrawesque toothiness, one scrutinizes the image for signs of slow death.

By 1983, Jimi, Janis and Jim, exorbitant, flaming comets, had crashlanded to be replaced by orbiting seventies survivors – Keith Richard, David Crosby, Eric Clapton, all the guys you wished had choked on their own vomit. Karen's death, conversely, belonged to pop, not rock. It was implosive, not explosive. She went out with a trooper's smile rather than a groupie's grope. Butabital, Dulcolax and thyroid pills, not coke or smack: these were her drugs, taken surreptiously rather than visibly. Her fugitive, chemical life emphasized the detached and oddly distanced air of both the Carpenters' records and their appearances. While a seventies audience praised their vulnerability and pathos, the eighties indie scene enjoyed the puppet-like blandness of the Carpenters, their similarity to virginal astronauts. All Todd Haynes's smart movie *Superstar* does is to literalize their awkwardness, their peculiarly Bambi-like hesitation in the form of real dolls.

Haynes directs Karen as a miserable Barbie doll, whittled down to a wire-thin sliver while Richard is a misogynst gay Ken who verbally abuses her. As the theme tune to *Superstar* plays, the Karen doll kneels with her head down the toilet and the Richard doll just stands there. Watching their smoothly impassive features implies both a familiarity with and a distrust of their smile, of the TV memory, a mood shared by Sonic Youth's 1990 track 'Tunic (Song For Karen)'. Kim Gordon sings from heaven, imagining herself as Karen looking down at earth: 'I feel like I'm disappearing/Getting smaller every day/I look in the mirror/And I'm bigger in every way.' Delivered in the most distant monotone possible, 'Song for Karen' suggests that the only way to sing a Carpenters' song is as a ruined elegy. *If I Was A Carpenter* never sounds as great as this because its ambitions are much smaller than Haynes's or Sonic Youth's.

The album immediately settles for a series of bedsit, guitar-heavy interpretations which miss both the lite futurism and the light entertainment aspects of their music. You get the feeling Shonen Knife

like 'Top of the World' because they can make a version that sounds like any other Shonen Knife song rather than something new that sounds like neither the former or the latter. They want to replace the cash tills the Carpenters had instead of hearts and replace their hovering, shimmering, studio-buffed sentimentality with guitars: more feeling, less predetermination – a naive notion since Richard's talent lay in grabbing a snatch of melody (he'd heard 'Close to You' as a jingle for a Crockers Citizens Bank advert), emphasizing its mass immediacy while twisting the genre into an orchestrally-lush widescreen mood. Hippies hated the ad-like manipulation of the Carpenters' commerciality. But for Americans, the Carpenters are as much a TV memory as an aural one. Between 1976 and 1981 they transmitted six TV specials and it's these repeats which have joined the nineties obsession with seventies FOSCs (family orientated situation comedies).

Nixon, conversely, loved the Carpenters for their corporate smoothness, their portable squareness. He based the idea of Reactionary Chic on the Carpenters and invited them to the Whitehouse in 1972, giving Richard a set of golf balls and cufflinks, and Karen a gold powder compact. Reactionary Chic meant sneering at the hippies as the new establishment in a language he'd learnt from them in the first place. It was a moment which would recur in the eighties over and over. Nixon used their isolation strategically, but the Carpenters themselves always behaved slightly out of time. Right up until she died, Karen would ask permission to swear, eating TV dinners while her husband dressed for a restaurant. If they'd been eighties kids they'd have their own chat show by now, co-hosted of course. If they'd been nineties kids they'd have their own book out entitled *How to Love Yourself and Be Successful.* Instead they toured incessantly, clung to each other with an intensity that frightened them, and polished their dreams of normality until they gleamed through each swelling string, each horn fanfare, each fragile breath Karen took.

(First published in *The Modern Review*, 1994.)

The Cold War

Cinema's obsession with post-War espionage resulted in some of the sixties' best moments, from Len Deighton's Harry Palmer trilogy (*The Ipcress File, Funeral In Berlin, Billion Dollar Brain*), through Bond, to spy thrillers such as *The Quiller*

The first and by far superior of Michael Caine's appearances as Len Deighton's Harry Palmer, Sidney J. Furie's 1965 adaptation of *The Ipcress File* is given extra weight by John Barry's sparse, yet spectacularly moving score. The Cold War would never seem so exotic

HARRY SALTZMAN Presents

MICHAEL CAINE

TOP SECRET

THE IPCRESS FILE

FROM THE NOVEL BY
LEN DEIGHTON

NIGEL GREEN · GUY DOLEMAN · SUE LLOYD
TECHNICOLOR® TECHNISCOPE®

PRODUCED BY
HARRY SALTZMAN · SIDNEY J. FURIE · CHARLES KASHER · BILL CANAWAY & JAMES DORAN · JOHN BARRY

Memorandum and Dean Martin's Matt Helm spoofs. The classic secret service soundtrack came complete with sombre strings, muted horns and giddy xylophones.

classic

Ray Coniff
'Music To Watch Girls By' (2.57)
Album: It Must Be Him (CBS) 1970

A song which, like many in the easy canon, has its roots firmly in the music of Latin America, in terms of tempo, arrangement and production. A preposterous take on the battle of the sexes, this sixties staple has been covered by James Last, Floyd Cramer, Geoff Love, you name them. *This,* however, is the definitive version, a positively life-affirming one at that.

Left: 'Instead of playing trombone solos that other musicians liked, I made an about-face and wrote my arrangements with a view to making the masses understand and buy records,' says Ray Coniff. 'From that point, I became very successful. I use the word "success" both financially and as a person'

classic

Elvis Costello
'I Wanna Be Loved' (5.36)
Single (F. Beat) 1984

This Ricky Nelson cover has all the requisite MOR staples, including a blistering, OTT keyboard refrain, while the extended-play version is blessed with a rather grand echo. Gorgeous. (Incidentally, the opening chord echoes the beginning of 10cc's 'I'm Not In Love'.)

Above: Elvis Costello has collaborated with many people, including Paul McCartney, Billy Sherrill, Robert Wyatt, James Burton and Burt Bacharach, and has always expressed a penchant for classic middle-of-the-road songwriting ('Oliver's Army', one of his biggest early hits, was based around a refrain borrowed from ABBA)

'Bobby Darin looked right at home in a lounge, wearing his white dinner jacket and bow tie,' says R.J. Smith. 'But then Darin always looked at home, whether in Vegas or in experimental movies like *Pressure Point*, whether singing in a Catskill supper club or simply on *American Bandstand*'

classic

Bobby Darin
'Beyond The Sea' (2.42)
Single (London) 1960
The chameleon-like fifties teen idol reinvented himself towards the end of the decade with a series of grown-up cover versions, including 'Mack The Knife', 'Lazy River' and 'Nature Boy', as well as this remarkable adaptation of Charles Trenet's 1945 standard 'La Mer'. 'Somewhere . . .'

classic

Ray Davies & the Button-Down Brass
'Up, Up And Away' (2.10)
Album: 16 Star Tracks (Philips) 1971
Not the Kinks' frontman, but the almost as legendary sixties trumpeter, here excelling himself on a rather punky (accelerated) cover of Jimmy Webb's soaring signature tune. Recorded in 1968, it includes drumming which would shame the Buzzcocks' John Maher, who didn't come on the scene till a good eight years later.

classic

Carolyn Dee
'Masquerade' (3.58)
Album: The Spy With The Platinum Heart (Disques Noir) 1987
Taken from a marvellous spoof spy soundtrack recorded by the Brian Marshall Orchestra & Chorus (Hey!), this aspires to Nelson Riddle and John Barry and feels like the aural equivalent of an Anton Corbijn photograph. Worlds within worlds, indeed.

Martin Denny
by Sally Holloway

Question: What do blockbusting novelist James Michener, *Magnificent Seven* director John Sturges and legendary newspaper columnist Walter Winchell have in common? Answer: all three wrote eulogistic sleevenotes for Martin Denny, the King of Exotica. Now aged eighty-four, semi-retired and living in Honolulu, the great bandleader is unabashed. 'In my career,' he says, 'I have received nothing but accolades.'

In his heyday of the late fifties and sixties, Martin Denny produced thirty-seven LPs of exotic mood music for Liberty Records, selling over four million copies. In 1959 – the year in which his first LP, *Exotica*, hit number one in the US charts and his single 'Quiet Village' made number two – Britain was too busy rocking out to Tommy Seele to notice. Although most of his records were available in the UK, post-War America's love affair with Martin Denny and Tiki culture never really caught on in Britain.

Years later, Martin Denny was discovered by such unlikely devotees as Genesis P Orridge and composer Steve Beresford, both of whom came across his music during sojourns on the West Coast. 'This was thrift store music, records my friends' parents had thrown out for Richard Clayderman,' says Beresford. 'Except it was better than that and they didn't realize.'

'When my music first emerged, some people thought it bizarre,' says Denny. An unapologetic cocktail of Hawaiian melodies, Latin rhythms, and all-American sentiments, Denny's music has been described as 'apple pie with a hint of mango'. Denny uses his own analogy: 'If you've ever tried half a papaya and put a scoop of passion fruit in it, it's a marvellous taste. My music is like that, an exotic fruit salad.'

A classically-trained pianist, Martin Denny arrived in Hawaii in 1954 to play solo piano at the Don the Beachcomber bar in Waikiki. Later he formed a jazz trio which became a quartet. It was while playing the open-air Shell Bar of the Hawaiian Village nightclub that Denny developed his unique sound – almost by accident. 'There was a park near our stage in which there were these bull frogs,' he recalls. 'One night we were playing there and I noticed this croaking all through the performance. Some of the boys in the band got carried away and started doing bird calls. The following day, somebody walked up to me and said, "Mr Denny, you know that song you did with the birds and the frogs? Can you do that again?" I thought, What are you talking about?, but I suddenly realized he had a point.' From then on, obliging band members found themselves performing extraordinary animal sounds to order.

Denny next developed an interest in strange instruments. Whenever friends travelled abroad they were deputized to bring back whatever they could find. 'I utilized these things however I could,' says Denny. 'For instance, for "Hello, Young Lovers", instead of using a regular bass I would build it around the sound of the big gongs that I had. So when you watched it onstage, there was pure visual entertainment as well as the music. People were elated by that.'

Denny followed up *Exotica* with a succession of LPs whose titles similarly evoke a Hawaiian beach paradise: *Primitiva*, *Hypnotique*, *Romantica*. His popularity reached critical mass in the mid-sixties. 'My music was used by choreographers for ballet, in Chinese and Polynesian

Top: Ray Davies: not a Kink in sight, only a rather brash trumpet

Bottom: Carolyn Dee, the spy who came on with a cold

'Why do I go for Martin Denny's type of music?' asked James A. Michener in the sleeve notes to Denny's *Hawaii*. 'It uses instruments and rhythms most usually found in popular music. It's witty, and much to the taste of people who like a little humour for the long haul'

restaurants, and even in Disneyland.' Sadly, his last work, *Exotica '90*, recorded for the Japanese market, is not his best. 'I repeated some of the things I had done before, except with new technology. Frankly, it lacked the feeling of my earlier works. You can't go home again, you know.'

Little of Denny's work has been available in the UK recently, except in the tattered easy-listening sections of the second-hand record shops, but now Creation subsidiary Rev-ola has released a compilation of his work.

How does Denny view his late-found cult status? Now happily ensconced in his Honolulu condominium with his wife June and their toy poodle, he is pleased but unimpressed. 'I've no idea what impression my music has made in Britain. Maybe it's taken all this time for people to catch on.' Aloha, as they say.

(First published in *Mojo*, 1995.)

Martin Denny

'Exotique Bossa Nova' (2.20)
Album: The Versatile Martin Denny (Liberty) 1966
Hawaii, the lad. A mesmerizing example of Denny's surreal marriage of quiet jazz and psychedelic sound-effects: finger cymbals, bamboo sticks, congas, sea birds etc.

Esquivel

by Irwin Chusid

They call it Space-age pop – and no one did it better than Juan Garcia Esquivel.

One reviewer called him a 'walking contradiction – a pop *avant-gardist*.' *Variety* proclaimed: 'Esquivel is to pop music approximately what Aaron Copland is to serious music or what a John Coltrane is to jazz.' A music critic declared: 'He copies no one . . . Conventional he ain't.' And one journalist tagged him 'the Busby Berkeley of Cocktail Music'.

Esquivel was a multi-threat talent: quirky composer, eccentric arranger, enchanting performer, dashing showman – a Paganini for the jet set.

For many, the words 'big band' conjure up nostalgic images of Glenn Miller serenading a dance hall with honeysweet renditions of swing era chestnuts. Esquivel scored his sets for the ballrooms of Venus. Scattered amid the piano and trombones were whip-smart slide guitar, dense echo and post-bebop rhythmic ricochet; a dose of dissonance; unearthly percussion, and weird juxtapositions of mood and volume. In a split second, his twenty-six piece orchestra could downshift from *caliente* to *fresco*. Esquivel's ingenious approach incorporated Chinese bells, organ, harpsichord, bass accordion, Jew's harp and mariachi strings, often over a bed of bongos. Clearly, not grandma's music.

What Esquivel couldn't squeeze out of brass, he conjured up with the Ondioline (an early electronic keyboard that offered an odd array of pitches); the ghostly theremin (popularized in the Hitchcock film *Spellbound*); and the Buzzimba, described as 'a one-of-a-kind instrument that is struck with mallets and sounds like a low-register resonant clarinet'. *Un amigo* coined the term 'Sonorama' (a play on 'panorama') to describe the maestro's sonic palette; Esquivel liked the word's 'futuristic' cachet.

He was, foremost, an arranger. 'It's a job title nearly extinct in today's music industry,' observed Dave Nuttycombe, of the *Washington City*

Paper. 'Arranging is largely an intellectual process, done with no musicians in sight. Working with a pencil and blank sheets of staff paper, the arranger draws in trumpet notes at the sixth measure, eases violins out by the twelfth. It can be as passionless as a mathematics problem. As his unorthodox sonic combinations reflect, Esquivel clearly brought intensity to the task.'

In (re)arranging Tin Pan Alley standards, he'd mischievously stray far from the melody, then unexpectedly assert the original theme. He replaced well-known lyrics with whistling, humming, or a disjointed phrase, creating a soundscape at once familiar yet utterly foreign. His smooth choruses (often the Randy Van Horne Singers) would croon 'Zu-zu-zu', or belt out 'Pow! Pow!!' He also composed campy pop tunes like 'Whatchamacallit', 'Mini Skirt', and 'Mucha Muchacha'.

Esquivel was a perfectionist and a sophisticated audio alchemist (wtih a degree in engineering from the University of Mexico). An expert in microphone placement, he arrived in the US in the late fifties, just as stereo LPs began hitting shops, and his arrangements took full advantage of the revolution in sound. Yet, despite a reliance on state-of-the-art studio gimmicks and the intense discipline his charts imposed on musicians, there was tremendous passion and abundant humour in Esquivel's music. His piano artistry was aggressive, yet elegant, with a virtuoso command of dynamic extremes.

'Where are you from?' a San Francisco club patron once asked Esquivel after a spellbinding performance. With a sly grin, the bandleader replied, 'Some people say I'm from Mars.'

The possibility of a Martian bloodline notwithstanding, his birth certificate says Tampico, Tamaulipas, Mexico, on 20 January 1918. His family moved to Mexico City when Juan was ten. The young prodigy showed a flair for the keyboard and electronics. (As a boy, he contrapted a primitive radio using lead ore, antenna wire and headphones.) By the age of fourteen, he was a featured soloist on XEW, the city's most popular radio station. At eighteen, he was composing, arranging and conducting his own twenty-two piece band. Through his constant exposure in theatres, on radio (often eight broadcasts per week) and on the concert stage, he attained immense popularity in his homeland.

A restless experimenter, Esquivel added new instruments to his radio band until, by the early fifties, he had amassed a fifty-four piece orchestra. He looks back on this phase of his career with a raised eyebrow. 'The radio shows were live, so you had no control where the musicians were concerned,' he recalls. 'If we had rehearsal on Friday until two in the afternoon, some of the musicians would then go to a bar and drink right up to show time. The result would sometimes be disastrous.'

Left: A walking contradiction – a pop avant-gardist – Esquivel is to popular music approximately what Aaron Copland is to 'serious' music or what John Coltrane is to jazz. He was also somewhat of a babe-hound, and courted a long and uninterrupted succession of beautiful and famous women

This taught him a lesson: great conductors must occasionally be great dictators. (This insight was later codified in 'The Regulations and Bylaws to Belong to the Esquivel Organization', which all talent was required to sign. Fines were imposed on dancers who gained weight, musicians who arrived late for rehearsals and performers who got married without giving advance notice.)

Along with Luis Alcaraz and Perez Prado, Esquivel was one of the most popular and hardest-working orchestra leaders in Mexico. Besides his radio shows and concert dates, he scored and appeared in two feature films, *Cabaret Tragico* and *The Madness of Rock & Roll*. His first album, *Las Tandas de Juan Garcia Esquivel*, was released in Mexico around 1956; it consisted of two sides of continuous, unbanded dance selections.

Esquivel was the complete enchilada: he composed, bedazzled from the concert stage, and, with his undeniable charisma, charmed the ladies. (To this date, there is some dispute over how many times he's been married: Esquivel tells interviewers four times, while others insist it was three. He also has a son, Mario, but may not have married the mother.)

By the late fifties, the dawn of the space age, Esquivel was ready to explore other worlds. He was brought to Hollywood in 1958 by RCA Victor producer-manager Herman Diaz, Jr. 'Stereo was just getting launched,' Diaz recalled in a 1995 interview, 'and I felt his arranging and conducting skills were perfect for showcasing with the new technology.'

His first US release, *To Love Again*, had been recorded monophonically (a flat, one-dimensional process) in Mexico in 1957. The album is an interesting historical footnote, illustrating the emerging, but not fully developed, Sonorama magnificence. The liner notes describe Esquivel's 'dashing appearance' and the 'tasteful elegance of his clothes.' 'As for Esquivel's romantic life,' the notes revealed, 'fortune has amply blessed this good-looking young Latin American – there has been a long and uninterrupted succession of names of beautiful and famous women mentioned in connection with him.' (In a 1994 interview with *The Wire*, Esquivel reminisced, 'I have many loves in my life – music, cars, women and the piano. But not necessarily in that order.')

His second US release – his first in stereo – *Other Worlds, Other Sounds* was recorded in Hollywood in 1958 with a twenty-six piece orchestra and the Van Horne Singers. The album's astonishing range of musical textures, along with cover art depicting a scantily-clad lunar nymph cavorting amid moon craters, dramatically established his unique persona in a field then commonly known as 'instrumental pop'.

Randy Van Horne recalled his first recording date with Esquivel. 'When they hired me,' he explained, 'I didn't know Juan's music, and was surprised when I heard it. He did all the vocal arrangements himself. The use of "zu-zu-zu" and "pow! pow!" were pretty much his inventions. We walked in and had pages handed to us for sight-reading. At first I thought, "This is a piece of cake, it's so easy." But when I heard what the orchestra was playing, it was Panicsville. He'd write a simple C chord for us, but we were coming in on top of a G-flat or a D-flat. We couldn't easily find our notes. Fortunately, we happened to be attuned to the dissonant parts in jazz, so we could cut it.'

Four Corners of the World (1958), hastily recorded with studio time left over from the *Other Worlds* sessions, was next. It spotlighted Esquival on piano in a flute-guitar-bass-and-drums setting (check out 'April in Portugal'). 'I wasn't very happy with the recording because it was improvised,' he recalled. 'It didn't have the sound and quality of the *Other Worlds* arrangements.' Fortunately, his next two vinyl offerings – *Exploring New Sounds in Stereo* (1959, released in mono as *Exploring New Sounds in Hi-Fi*) and *Strings Aflame* (1959) – shifted back into warp drive. ('Malgueña' is a standout track from the latter.)

Based in New York for a year, he contributed a half-dozen spectacular arrangements to a multi-artist RCA Victor compilation entitled *The Merriest of Christmas Pops* (1959), and arranged and conducted *Hello, Amigos* (1960) for the Ames Brothers vocal quartet. Unbeknownst to many (then and now), he also conducted an album, *In a Mellow Mood*, released under the name the Living Strings. 'Mellow' is an overstatement – it's largely snooze-muzak. Esquival goes uncredited on the sleeve, though his distinctive piano runs punctuate the lush strings.

Back in Hollywood, our jet-set gaucho zoomed into overdrive with *Infinity in Sound* (1960) and – one of the pinnacles of his recording career – *Infinity in Sound, Vol 2* (1961). Neely Plumb, who produced these and other Esquivel albums, recalled his astonishment at the maestro's approach to 'the business of sound': 'We were absolutely electrified with the impact of what Juan would do with orchestration, and his impeccable patience and unending determination in the re-recording [mixing] process. God only knows how long it would take to remix. No matter how good it was, we'd finish making a tape, and I'd say, "How's that Juan?" And he'd politely say, "It's very good . . . (pause) . . . Let's make another one." And another one. Time and time again. Finally he'd say, "That's it!" That's when I would find something wrong! But the end product was worth it.

'There were no overdubs, no parts fixed. Overdubbing was a process that developed later. For this, we had mixing, equalizing, and above all, the addition of reverb-echo and all that. When it came out, we had a very live piece of merchandise.'

Fans of pioneering TV comedian Ernie Kovacs will note that

'Sentimental Journey' was used in a famous video sketch in which Kovacs choreographed office furniture and secretarial equipment to the music. Another Kovacs video, featuring kitchen appliances and a dancing stuffed turkey, used Esquivel's recording of 'Cherokee', also from *Vol. 2*.

Esquivel earned Grammy nominations in the Orchestral Recording category three years running: for *Other Worlds, Other Sounds* (1958), *Strings Aflame* (1959), and *Infinity in Sound* (1960). The same three albums were also nominated in the Engineering category. Although Esquivel didn't win top honours in any final balloting, placed behind such illustrious contemporaries as Sinatra, Mancini, and Billy May, it should be noted that *Other Worlds* lost the 1958 Engineering grammy to the foremost exponents of Rodent Rock – the Chipmunks.

Latin-Esque (1962) is, in the opinion of many, Esquivel's wildest and most ambitious effort. It was part of RCA Victor's Stereo Action series, a tour-de-force of twin-channel wizardry, touted as 'the sound your eyes can follow'. The album showcased a supersonic array of channel-to-channel panning, as pianos and percussion bounced from speaker to speaker, with generous washes of 'infinite tape reverberation'. To ensure pure stereo separation during the recording, half the orchestra was stationed in RCA's Hollywood Studio 1 under the baton of Esquivel, with the other half at Studio 2 – a block away – under guest conductor Stanley Wilson. The musicians were synchronized by 'click tracks' heard over headphones, and the conductors co-ordinated via closed-circuit television.

Throughout his years at RCA, Esquivel had a budget-be-damned attitude. No detail was too extravagant or too costly – especially with RCA's money. 'He was a perfectionist – always,' Diaz recalled. 'He made some very expensive records. Beautiful – but expensive.' Yet, Esquivel told *Music Guide*'s Cory Brown in 1995, 'RCA was very nice to me. They allowed me to experiment. If I wanted to record the orchestra using drapery behind the trumpets to soften the sound, they would allow me. If I wanted to record the violins with wooden floors beneath to brighten the sound, they would allow me. I could do whatever I wanted.'

Nevertheless, when his contract expired in 1962, Esquivel left the label to record *More of Other Worlds, Other Sounds* for Reprise Records.

Then, at the zenith of his record-making powers, the hotter-than-jalapeño bandleader went on studio hiatus for five years.

During this period, he developed his stage show, 'The Sights and Sounds of Esquivel', in Lake Tahoe and Las Vegas. Throughout his career, he was an exciting and critically lauded nightclub attraction, particularly in Vegas, where he had twenty-six week contracts with the Stardust Hotel. A July 1964 review of a San Francisco date at Bimbo's 365 Club noted that the stage show included a lighting technician 'who creates dramatic effects . . . precisely timed'. (This was, it should be pointed out, several years before Bay Area psychedelic bands took the technique to mind-melting extremes.) The dapper señor was known to change tuxedos a dozen times during an evening's performance.

In 1965, Esquivel auditioned a talented young Latin percussionist, singer and dancer named Yvonne DeBourbon. She joined his ensemble, eventually taking over his business affairs from 1969 to 1975. 'I managed the entire show,' DeBourbon recalled. 'I did the contracts and moved the show – 1,500 pounds of equipment and the entire entourage – all over the world.' (That wasn't all: in 1973, she became his wife.) A reviewer who caught the stage act during this period praised Esquivel's 'musical innovations and melodic humour', and noted the 'animation' of the 'wild comedy duets between his piano and the percussion of Adolfo Calderon'.

In the midst of an extended 1967 nightclub run at the Stardust, the tireless performer returned to the RCA studios to record *The Genius of Esquivel*. The album featured his pared-down Vegas combo rather than a big band; nonetheless, it projected a powerful musical force, as illustrated on 'Question Mark' and 'Flower Girl From Bordeaux'. His last RCA Victor project, *Esquivel 1968*, was released only in Mexico and Puerto Rico.

While in Hollywood, Esquivel composed soundtracks for the TV programmes *Markham*, *The Bob Cummings Show*, and *The Tall Man*. He also recorded for Universal Television countless short 'mood' pieces, which have been used in the soundtracks of TV sitcoms, dramas and adventure programmes ever since. For decades, Esquivel melodies have invaded your subconscious through such Nielsen-leaders as *The A-Team*, *Baretta*, *Baywatch*, *The Bionic Woman*, *Columbo*, *Dragnet*, MTV's *House of Style*, *Ironside*, *Kojak*, *Marcus Welby, MD*, *Miami Vice*, *The Munsters*, *Murder She Wrote*, *Night Gallery*, *Northern Exposure*, *Quincy*, *The Rockford Files* and *The Six Million Dollar Man*.

Esquivel and DeBourbon were divorced in 1978, after which he moved back south of the border. His next project was to compose and record themes for a children's TV puppet show called *Burbujas* ('bubbles'). Two albums were released in Mexico: *Burbujas* and *Odisea Burbujas*.

In July, 1993, Esquivel was visiting his brother, Sergio, in the Mexican town of Cuernavaca. While emerging from a taxi, he fell and broke his hip, aggravating an old spinal injury. He has been confined to bed at Sergio's home ever since.

Esquivel's orginal RCA Victor albums coincided with an era when rock'n'roll groups eclipsed orchestras as the standard-bearers of pop. Nevertheless, his atomic age mood music carried over into the rock sphere; overtones can be heard in the clever Beach Boys arrangements by Brian Wilson, in the monumental density of Phil Spector's 'Wall of

Sound', and in the Latin percussion inflections of Steely Dan. Yet, for all his record sales and legions of fans worldwide, Esquivel left no followers. His style was too idiosyncratic (*iy muy costoso!*) to emulate. After he retired from the recording studio and the bandstand, the suave señor left behind a vast vinyl legacy, which all-too-quickly went out of print. These days his original albums are extremely difficult to locate, having become high-priced collector's trophies.

Now, a new generation, hungry for a musical alternative to alternative music, has rediscovered the Mexican maestro's sublime Sonorama. 'Esquivel changed my life,' explained Michael 'The Millionaire' Cudahy, Combustible Edison guitarist. 'The first time I heard him I realized that this is my favourite kind of music.' Fred Schneider of the B-52s testified that 'Esquivel was way ahead of his time and should be heard now to give arrangers and producers some lessons.' And avant-saxophonist John Zorn called Esquivel 'a genius arranger who created a beautiful pop mutation'.

Though incapacitated, Esquivel hopes – and the world shares this hope – that his condition is temporary. 'I've been thinking of the possibilities of recording nowadays,' he mused. 'I'm just so full of ideas.' He misses the US. And he would love once again to indulge his great passions: music, cars, women and the piano – if not necessarily in that order.
(First published as the liner notes for the 1996 LP *Cabaret Mañana*.)

Exotica
by RJ Smith

It was 1956, and the damned bullfrog wouldn't shut up.

Pondside at the Shell Bar in an island joint called Hawaiian Village, pianist Martin Denny and his band were entertaining the tourists with the essential cocktail mix – light vibraphones, bongos, tropical lilt. They played their usual set, but . . . this . . bullfrog was making like Don Ho. It was a pain at first, but over the course of the evening the musicians swung with it, joining in with their own nature calls, mostly tropical bird songs that made the tropical tunes seem even further away. This was a key moment in musical history.

A year later Denny's hit recording of Les Baxter's 'Quiet Village' spearheaded a sound and style that called itself 'Exotica'. All praise to Baxter, and thanks to Denny, but let's not forget to kiss the frog.

Exotica was a round-trip ticket departing everyday for something more fabulous. It had the feel of distant places, but it took you to spots never before trekked by man, places that didn't exist except in the minds of musicians busily mangling Polynesian folk tunes, Chinese scales, Arabic harmonics and Indian instruments. Folkloric verisimilitude was not what they accomplished, nor even really what they had in mind. This music was as wonderfully bogus as a puu-puu platter, Suzy Wong or Thor Heyerdahl. This was better than the truth.

We start with Martin Denny, the high potentate of exotica. He was the concept man, the guy who saw how far he could ride on exotica's ticket. Denny's band was a string of rhinestones – vibraphonist Julius Wechter went on to form the Baja Marimba Band, Arthur Lyman would lead his own exotica ensemble, Augie Colon was the bongoman who talked to the birds. Denny's album covers featured the enticing Sandy Warner, also known as 'the exotica girl'. With his orchid-print cocktail band, Denny spread the word around the world. The music, too was restless, hopping from the Camel-cigarette Middle Easternisms of 'Misirlou' to the bungle-in-the-jungle drums of 'Jungle Madness', to the trancey, downward-spiralling 'Hypnotique' replete with sixties-specific sitar.

The late fifties to mid sixties was exotica's commercial apex, but it began long before. Exotica was born when soldiers returned from World War II's Pacific theatre with a taste for the South Pacific. National Geographic's subscription rate was ballooning, in rough proportion perhaps to the number of times they showed naked Samoan women posing before their huts. Tiki bars, apartment complexes, bowling alleys, liquor stores and mobile homes, all with a Polynesian flare, popped up everywhere. Restaurants with names like the Bahooka and the Luau and great chains like Don the Beachcomber's and Trader Vic's were booming successes. The mixological arts suddenly seemed alchemical as barkeeps fixed flaming concoctions served in skull-shaped mugs. Anthropologists have long noted the human disdain for blue food, but blue drinks were an invitation to excess.

Exotica is a world of white magic, red sunsets and golden showers

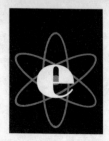

All this cultural production promised a world more primitive and less mediated than life in the burgeoning white collar states. Exotica was more than a sound, it was a design movement, and a pop art reaction to a Cold War paradigm that said all that was evil and deviate lurked barely outside our sacred borders. 'Let's cross over!,' exotica replied.

Every theology needs its prophet, though, and exotica was lucky to have Les Baxter. In the forties he was a jazz tenor saxophonist and singer with Mel Torme's *Mel-Tones*. But the sounds he had in mind – the wailings of flayed divas, the eerie croon of electronic instruments, the grunt of pleasure domes and jungle drums – couldn't fit on any big band playlist. Baxter was the first recording artist to make use of the theremin, and the only soundtrack composer to write music for films by Ingmar Bergman and Ed Wood. But his greatest success was with exotica, a form that wouldn't exist unless Baxter willed it into being.

There wasn't an excess imaginable that Baxter couldn't enfold in a nimbus of strings. Consider Bas Sheva, the trained cantor he hired to sing on *The Passions*. Dating from a moment when composers wrote song cycles evoking perfume scents, colours and masterpiece paintings, Bas Sheva's *The Passions* was meant to explore the many moods of *la femme*.

'Here is a challenge to the listener,' the liner notes puff. 'A powerful conception that plumbs the depths of human emotion. Here is a picture of a woman's passion painted with strokes of shocking brilliance . . . vital music written and performed with bold imagination . . . daringly executed for those who can sustain the most stimulating of listening sensations.' Before you take Les up on the challenge, better listen to 'Lust', with enough batty ululations to scare the flood pants off any cold warrior. At a time when passions seethed subterranean channels, Bas Sheva was so out in the open she must have been singing in italics.

Baxter's genius was for bending other peoples' sounds to meet his particular needs. 'Pyramid Of The Sun', after all, turns a human-sacrificing Aztec culture into a friendly tone poem. 'Voodoo Dreams/Voodoo', has more in common with the drink known as the 'Zombie' than with the animated corpse of *vodou* legends.

Perhaps the main focus of exotica's fascination was Hawaii, which had become a state in 1959. There was a craze for all things evoking our new dominion; 'how could something so foreign be part of us?' we wondered. 'How could we enfold it into the American body? The Out-Islanders' 'Moon Mist' and Webley Edwards's 'Alika' point to one answer: treat the islands like the latest Disneyland attraction, a quality-controlled environment ripe for tourist dollars.

The exotica movement thrived into the mid sixties and then vanished. As global travel became cheaper and quicker, the exploits of the armchair explorer seemed less meaningful. Or perhaps the Vietnam war killed the allure; the fun went out of getting soused in make-believe third-world huts when elsewhere napalm rained down on real huts. But without a context today – few even remember the exotica heyday – this music seems more wonderful than ever, and its powers to take you to other dimensions oddly amplified. This is an art music that time forgot. Let's cross over.

(First published as the liner notes for the 1996 LP *Mondo Exotica*.)

Percy Faith

A champion of sweet violins and carnivorous brass, he could turn simple melodic lines into full-scale orchestrations at the drop of a wide-band hat, becoming more than a little bit famous for his rendition of the Max Steiner classic 'Theme From *A Summer Place*' as well as albums such as *Themes For Young Lovers* (1962). In 1950 he described his goal as being that of 'satisfying the millions of devotees of that pleasant American institution known as the quiet evening at home, whose idea of perfect relaxation is the easy chair, slippers and good music.' Bless.

Left: He was born Clive Powell in 1943, and was the earliest British exponent of the Hammond organ, blasting out 'Yeh Yeh' and 'Get Away' before being lured down the middle of the road. Once there he recorded extraordinary things like 'Because I Love You' and 'I Didn't Want To Have To Do It'

Above: 'Percy Faith's delicate balance between being too mellow and too raucous was both a musical gift and a career scourge,' says Joseph Lanza. 'On the one hand he was a champion of sweet violins; but on the other, he always grew skittish when his reputation got too caught up in them'

classic

Georgie Fame

'Try My World' (2.23)
Single (Columbia) 1967
After he emerged as an R&B performer, and before he turned into a suburban cabaret act, Fame recorded some excellent easy tunes (much against his better judgement), including this over-orchestrated piece of lush life, as well as 1969's beautiful 'Hideaway' and 'Peaceful' (later covered rather badly by Helen Reddy).

classic

The Fifth Dimension

'Stoned Soul Picnic' (3.23)
Album: Greatest Hits On Earth (Arista) 1972
The Fifth's late sixties 'psychedelic soul' was heavily sugar-coated, and they became famous largely because of their soaring vocal harmonies. This is one of their many Laura Nyro covers (the others include 'Wedding Bell Blues' and 'Save The Country'); to paraphrase Brian Eno, 'So economical and clear in its intentions and results.'

Guy Fletcher & Douglas Flett

'At last I know,
Those in love are never free,
But free was what I had to be,
And so – I cut the ties that bind,
And slipped away . . . leaving something fine . . .

'. . . I'm high, I'm high,
Yes lately I've been doing fine,
Though I think of you from time to time,
In truth you're seldom off my mind,
But I lost you . . . somewhere down the line'

'Somewhere Down The Line' by Guy Fletcher and Douglas Flett, 1979

Fletcher/Flett, a two-man Brill Building: 'I Can't Tell The Bottom From The Top', 'Just Pretend', 'Blue Boy', 'Simple Affair Of The Heart', 'Fallen Angel', 'Goodbye Birds', 'The Fair's Moving On', 'Somewhere Down The Line', 'Save Me', 'One Nation', 'Is There Anyone Out There?', 'Lady, Put The Light Out' etc

Few songwriting partnerships have lasted as long as Fletcher/Flett, who for thirty years have been carving out power ballads, pop-rock torch songs and R&B and country tunes with the dedication of true craftsmen. Inspired by the Beatles and the Beach Boys, they came together in the mid-sixties – Australian-born Flett from the advertising industry, Fletcher from the Joe Meek school of pop – disciplining themselves to write hit records by the yard; something they did with unerring success. They have written hits in almost every genre, whilst also involving themselves in musicals, commercials, production and publishing. Their forte – like Bacharach and David, and Brian Wilson before them – has always been off-kilter ballads – deceptively simple songs which can break your heart at forty paces: 'Fallen Angel' (Frankie Valli), 'The Fair's Moving On' and 'Just Pretend' (both Elvis Presley), 'I Can't Tell The Bottom From The Top' (the Hollies), 'Is There Anyone Out There?' (Ray Charles), 'Lady, Put The Light Out' and the agonizingly heartfelt 'Somewhere Down The Line' – both recorded by Rogue, a studio band

71

fronted by Fletcher, which also included Alan Hodge and John Hodkinson, who released three LPs from 1976 to 1979. There are dozens of others, including Fletcher's own version of their effortless folk-tinged ballad 'Boy Blue' (which knocks Paul Weller and Nick Drake into a cocked straw boater), 'Goodbye Birds', and more recently, 'Mercy', 'A Simple Affair Of The Heart' and 'It's A Jungle Out There'. Though they have never really been away, they are currently experiencing serious re-evaluation. Their 18-carat classic, a neglected would-be standard – remains 'Somewhere Down The Line' ('A love so strong, is given to the lucky few/And fills the very heart of you/You know, we're two of a kind/But we let it go . . . somewhere down the line'), while Fletcher's two solo LPs, *Guy Fletcher* (Philips, 1971) and *When The Morning Comes* (Philips, 1972) contain some of their most enduring collaborations. Fletcher has recently recorded a third solo album featuring old and new Fletcher/Flett compositions.

Like Eurotunnel is a fifties idea of the future (see *The Nightfly* by Donald Fagen), so the Gentle People portray a world that would have been impossible without the flagrant optimism of post-war America. You've never seen so many stores? Well, you have now

The Gentle People

Dougee Dimensional, Honeymink, Laurie LeMans and Valentine Carnelian sure give good press release: 'They have travelled from the outer reaches of the galaxy to the inner sanctum of your heart. They call this music easycore: utilizing the digital technology of today and the lost sounds of yesterday to create the music for the millennium generation.' Though they are part and parcel of Britain's burgeoning Cocktail Nation, the Gentle People produce easy listening for the techno brigade, a unique ambient sound – fromage collage, easy hard core? – that is genuinely extraordinary; as *Wired* said, 'it's as if Brigitte Bardot, the Aphex Twin and Jason King have all put on multicoloured fun-furs and jetted on to your patio for a fondue party'. Alternatively you could say they sound like a head-on collision between Brian Eno and Serge Gainsbourg, between *Barbarella* and *The Jetsons*.

Astrud Gilberto

For more than thirty years Astrud Gilberto has been singing the gentle, lyrical samba ballads of Brazil, a career which was kick-started by a happy accident in a New York recording studio in 1963. Early that year Stan Getz called up the celebrated Brazilian pianist Antonio Carlos Jobim, asking him to bring along some of his new material. Getz was looking to record the follow-up to *Jazz Samba* and *Jazz Samba Encore* – his two breakthrough LPs which had resulted in the hits 'Desafinado' (Slightly Out Of Tune) and 'Samba De Una Nota So' (One Note Samba). The sensual sun-kissed samba Jobim brought to the studio that day was 'The Girl From Ipanema'; he also brought along a friend, the guitarist Joao Gilberto. The song vividly showcased Getz's pure-toned tenor sax and the intimate, burry voice of Gilberto, though as recording progressed it became all-too evident that Gilberto could only sing in Portuguese, and was therefore unable to interpret the English lyrics written by Norman Gimbel. And so Getz asked Gilberto's twenty-four-year-old Bahia-born wife to sing it for him.

'I just happened to be in the studio that day,' says Astrud. 'I had never sung professionally before, but everything seemed to click.' Initially her contribution was considered so slight that she was not even credited on the resulting album, *Stan Getz/Joao Gilberto*, though stardom beckoned when an edited single version of the song went to number five on the US charts, staying on the nation's Hot 100 for three months.

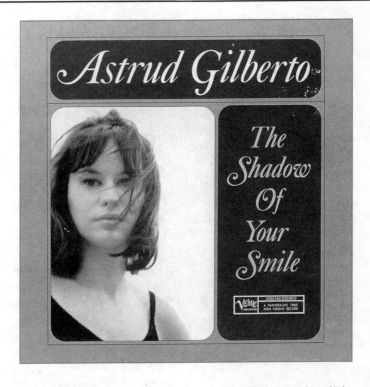

Astrud Gilberto, forever doomed to be captioned young, tall, tan, lovely etc

'I lived in Ipanema for twenty years,' she says. 'So I guess I *was* a girl from Ipanema, but not *the* girl – that girl could have been anyone, and it probably was. I love the song and I really don't mind if people associate it with me because it has become a standard. The bossa nova ['new wave'] has come to signify all the happy things in life: at the movies, whenever you hear a bossa nova song start to play, you know that the boy and girl are going to kiss. It's *so* sexy.'

Gilberto has since become synonymous with all that is filigree and sensual, and has covered every classic tune from 'Fly Me To The Moon' and 'Trains And Boats And Planes' through to 'It Might As Well Be Spring' and 'I Haven't Got Anything Better To Do'. The liner notes to her 1965 LP *The Shadow Of Your Smile* say it all: 'Astrud Gilberto . . . the sound of innocence remembered. A clear voice, light and graceful, weighted only with the soft haze of autumn moonlight. A voice that shares with you a sense of things *felt* rather than things *seen*. A voice filled with shadows and memory.'

Morton Gould

The esoteric, genre-bending band leader was around at the dawn of lounge, leading his dauntless orchestra through a series of experimental albums in the late fifties and early sixties as they traversed varied landscapes of style and persuasion: *Moon, Wind And Stars* (1958), *Jungle Drums* (1960) and *Blues In The Night* (1960).

Chris Gunning

'Try a taste of Martini,
The most beautiful drink in the world,
It's the bright one,
The right one,
It's Martini . . .'

'The so-called serious musicians turned up his or her nose at light music,' says Morton Gould. 'If you could be in a private club you could feel superior. There were a lot of psychological, physiological, and in some cases pathological reasons for these feelings'

Any time, any place, anywhere . . . Chris Gunning's iconic Martini theme is one of the advertising industry's most celebrated tunes, a song which – accompanied by images of multi-coloured hot air balloons, lovers walking hand-in-hand by the Golden Gate bridge and yachts careering along the Nice shoreline – is ingrained upon the public's consciousness.

His CV is startling: having recorded with Mel Tormé, Dudley Moore, Cilla Black, Colin Blunstone, the Hollies, Shirley Bassey and Tommy Steele, he moved into TV and film work, winning BAFTAs for *Middlemarch, Agatha Christie's Poirot* and *Porterhouse Blue* and an Ivor Novello Award for *Under Suspicion*. Most recently he scored the music for Dennis Potter's final works, *Karaoke* and *Cold Lazarus,* while his most powerful work remains *Yorkshire Glory,* a fifty-three-minute musical evocation commissioned by Yorkshire Television.

Such are his achievements that asking Gunning about his commercials

'McCann Erickson had this lyric which they needed to set to music, and the inspiration was meant to be Bacharach,' says the composer of the famous Martini tune, Chris Gunning. 'I wrote it in one night and it lasted twenty-five years. It was one of the first music-led campaigns to really take off, and was used all over the world'

career seems a little like asking Woody Allen about his 'earlier, funnier' films. Having worked as an arranger for the artists listed above, he was asked by Brian De Salvo – an advertising bigwig who happened to be moonlighting as a pop singer – if he had thought about working in commercials. He hadn't, but he soon did, scoring a theme for an ad for British United Airways. 'The catch phrase was The Jet Set Are Here! and I remember saying, Shouldn't it be The Jet Set Is Here? But I got nothing but stony looks from the copywriters. The music was all right, but I was absolutely gob-smacked at the amount of money I got. It seemed wicked.'

Over the next decade, Gunning was to score hundreds of commercials ('For just about every household item you can think of'), including work for Black Magic, Lloyds Bank, Kodak, Benson & Hedges, Canada Dry, Citroën, Dunhill, Ford, Land Rover, Polaroid, Nat West, Chanel No. 19 and Terry's All Gold. And, of course, Martini, in the spring of 1970. 'McCann Erickson had this lyric which they needed set to music, and the inspiration was meant to be Bacharach. I wrote it in one night and it lasted twenty-five years. It was one of the first music-led campaigns to really take off, and was used all over the world. I did about fifteen adaptations altogether, in styles from Sinatra to Vivaldi – sixty-second, forty-five, forty, thirty, twenty and ten – it was always a bugger doing the short ones.'

Such was the tune's success that it was turned into a full-blown instrumental ('The Right One'), a vocal version with a new middle-eight sung by Danny Williams, and even a French disco hit. 'It's been a blessing in many ways,' says Gunning, 'but a mixed one. It was financially very welcome at the time, though I'm not sure I'd like to do another!'

Françoise Hardy
by Bob Stanley

'I'm ashamed to say it but I've always had a problem with being famous. You can divide the human race between show-offs and voyeurs – I prefer to look at other people.' Françoise Hardy has to be the least egotistical superstar in the world. Following her collaborations with Blur and Malcolm McLaren, in 1996 she released a new album, *Le Danger*, some thirty-four years after her first single. 'Tous Les Garçons Et Les Filles', made when she was sixteen, sold a million copies in Europe and within months she was on the cover of *Paris Match*, singing in Eurovision, and starring in a Roger Vadim film.

'I came from a very respectable family and I didn't know much about life. I wrote my own songs, but just making a record seemed like reaching

Overleaf: Before she was caught by Catherine Deneuve, Françoise Hardy was the unofficial symbol of France, the epitome of cool elegance and style. And, unlike Deneuve, she could sing her little white cotton socks off

for the moon. I wasn't aware of what might happen-just as well, otherwise I would never have made a record.'

By 1965, her fame had reached Britain and the States – Bob Dylan was obsessed, and it's a safe bet that half of *Blonde on Blonde* was aimed at her. Mick Jagger laid siege to her Paris apartment to no avail. A photo circa 1966 shows the happy couple, the thwarted Jagger a good few inches shorter than Françoise. Under my thumb? I think not, monsieur.

The Hardy sound was often melancholic, sumptuously arranged and quite beautiful. Moreover, the music was wrapped in sleeves to die for, thanks to her boyfriend at the time, photographer Jean-Marie Perier. The album to track down is *Viens*, from 1971, a collaboration with Brazilian singer Tuca (they were rumoured to have had an affair). It features heartbreaking string arrangements and an incredibly intimate atmosphere. 'Chanson D'O', breathy and wordless, is possibly the most sensuous song ever recorded.

Still ultra-elegant and with a figure that earned her the unflattering nickname Asparagus, Françoise was recently tempted out of semi-retirement by some of her more famous fans. 'For me, working with Blur, it's like a dream. I was flicking through the TV channels one night and I caught the end of an interview with Damon. Well, I thought he seemed very nice. The following morning I got a fax from their record company saying they wanted to work with me on "To The End". It was like being in a playground.'

And then there was Malcolm McLaren and his ill-fated *Paris* album, a project Françoise wasn't quite so fond of. 'I don't like Malcolm McLaren. I don't like the way he works. We recorded an excellent song with a Phil Spector atmosphere I loved. When I heard the record he'd kept only my voice and given it a disco backing. A nightmare! I was ashamed. He's a crazy man.' Now we have *Le Danger* (Virgin), an album of guitar-heavy Francopop which won't appeal to the growing lounge/easy crowd, but Françoise cares not a jot. Just to be perverse, her next album could even be sung in-gulp-German. 'I spent a lot of childhood holidays in Austria. I think it's a very musical language.' If you detect a bierkeller influence on the next Blur album, you know who to blame.
(First published in *Arena*, 1996.)

Françoise Hardy
'All Over The World' (2.32)
Single (Pye) 1965
The Françoise Sagan of the seven-inch single, 'All Over The World' is one of her few English-language hits, a melancholy mix of Marianne Faithfull and Francis Lai. Tragic, in the true sense of the word.

classic

Richard Harris

'Macarthur Park' (7.20)

Single (RCA) 1968

Written and recorded as a bet (Webb won: it was a hit), 'Macarthur Park' is one of pop's great epics, ranking alongside 'Hey Jude', 'Layla' and 'Overnite Sensation'. Kitsch? For sure. Grandiose? Possibly. A towering achievement? Absolutely. Incidentally, the song apparently 'inspired' the Pearl & Dean cinema theme tune.

classic

Noel Harrison

'Windmills Of Your Mind' (2.14)

Single (Reprise) 1969

This Oscar-winning song first appeared in Norman Jewison's silly but stylish movie *The Thomas Crown Affair,* starring Steve McQueen and Faye Dunaway. The TV sitcom star Hannah Gordon once performed this to fine effect on *The Morecambe & Wise Show,* though this is the finest recorded version, by Rex's son, no less. '. . . never ending or beginning . . . on an ever-spinning wheel . . .'

Left: Along with Peter O'Toole and Richard Burton, Richard Harris was one of the sixties' true thespian 'wild children'-a great actor, a great boozer, and a not-as-bad-as-we-all-expected singer. 'I didn't exactly want to be a singer, but somehow at the time it just seemed like the right thing to do,' he says. 'I'm glad I did it then as I'm not so sure I could carry it off now. But, having said that . . .'

Below: To paraphrase Iggy Pop, Noel Harrison is the world's forgotten boy

79

Tony Hatch: No more Mr Nice Guy?
No more Mr Clean?

Tony Hatch

It could be a debilitating routine, the ultimate showbiz nightmare. 'So, Tony, marks out of ten for star quality?' The hopeful contestant would stand centre-stage, quivering like a cartoon whippet, waiting for the verdict. Like a malevolent Roman emperor, Tony Hatch would deliver the thumbs-down. 'Nought,' he would say, his face rigid and unsmiling. 'Nothing.'

For many, Tony Hatch will forever remain the 'Hatchet' man on ATV's Saturday-night talent show, *New Faces,* a kind of *Opportunity Knocks* with spunk which broke stars like Marti Caine and Showaddywaddy. During the seventies the show was infamous for Hatch's reliably heartless verdicts on the third-rate impressionists and sonically-challenged vocalists. Most notoriously he once gave the aspiring singer Malandra Burrows a resounding 'nought' for said star quality, seemingly oblivious to the fact that poor Malandra was only eight.

He had another reputation, too, for writing sickly-sweet soap-opera theme tunes, namely *Emmerdale, Neighbours* and *Crossroads* – though he deserves recognition for churning out dozens of classic pop songs and TV themes which in their own way rival anything by Bacharach.

Hatch cut his show-business teeth as a staff producer for Pye Records in the early sixties; the company were so desperate to sign him that they did so whilst he was still finishing his National Service, which took him into the band of the Coldstream Guards. 'It was a standing joke that for my first two years at Pye, they could only have meetings in the afternoon because I had to be on parade in the morning,' he says. At Pye he became Petula Clark's producer and supplied her with 'Downtown' and 'Don't Sleep In The Subway' amongst others, while writing the title tunes for TV programmes like *The Champions, Sportsnight, Hadleigh* and *Man Alive* (perhaps the quintessential sixties TV theme). He quickly earned friends and respect within the industry, and, as the *Sunday Times* journalist Simon Mills has pointed out, soon acquired more nicknames than James Brown, including Mr Versatility, Mr Music and – though this was almost certainly lost on Malandra Burrows' manager – Mr Nice Guy.

An entertainment journeyman, the worst you can say about Tony Hatch is that he wrote music for money, and if you delve into his back catalogue you will discover some perfectly-cut gems – including several songs he wrote and recorded with his ex-wife Jackie Trent – which deserve to be polished, mounted and kept in very dry, very secure places of worship.

Tony Hatch

'Man Alive' (2.00)
Album: Downtown With Tony Hatch (Pye) 1967
No one has written more great TV scores than the Hatchet – although admittedly no one has written more appalling ones, too. 'Man Alive' (1965) is one of his best, full of adrenaline, vibrancy and a ridiculous sense of urgency.

Isaac Hayes

By deliberately fusing soap opera and ghetto chic, in the late sixties and early seventies Isaac Hayes created his own, highly rhythmic, symphonic environment, and in his way was as influential as Sly Stone; both men moved away from R&B and into traditionally white areas: Stone into rock, Hayes into the orchestral world of Bacharach, Jimmy Webb and Carole King. The son of a Memphis sharecropper, Hayes joined Stax Records in 1964, aged twenty-two, eventually writing, arranging and producing dozens of hits for Sam and Dave, Carla Thomas and Johnnie Taylor ('Hold On I'm Coming', 'Soul Man', 'B-A-B-Y', etc.).

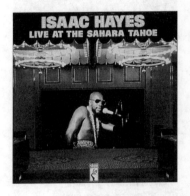

Who's the guy covered in all the old tom? Blimey, it's Isaac!

It was his 1969 solo LP *Hot Buttered Soul,* however, which really brought him personal acclaim. At the time it was cited as the most important black album since *James Brown Live At The Apollo* (1962), *Hot* included an eighteen-minute version of Jimmy Webb's 'By The Time I Get To Phoenix' and an elaborate reworking of Bacharach's 'Walk On By'. Hayes draped white bread orchestral arrangements around his seemingly interminable monologues, as though experimenting with various convoluted seduction techniques. With his lush raps and funereal beats, Hayes gave you the impression he could turn a thirty-second hairspray ad into a three-hour symphony complete with several different movements and at least a dozen costume changes.

He had – still has, in fact – a dark brown crooner's voice which perfectly suited the type of rich ballads which became his forte: 'It's Too Late', 'Windows Of The World', 'The Look Of Love', 'Ain't No Sunshine', etc. He was a remarkable arranger, and the bulk of his 1971 LP *Shaft* – in which he reached critical mass while winning two Grammys and an Oscar – is almost worthy of Bernard Herrmann. But self-absorption was only just around the corner, hovering like a stalker in the rain. The records became more bombastic – check out his bizarre 1977 duet with Dionne Warwick (*A Man And A Woman*) and the kitsch-in-sink extravaganza that is 1973's *Live At The Sahara Tahoe* – as Hayes's personal life became more extreme.

Die-hard libidinist, funky Renaissance man, Hayes preferred the Black

Moses monicker: he delivered. Talking about *Hot Buttered Soul,* he said recently: 'Like rock groups, I always wanted to present songs as dramas – it was something white artists did so well but black folks hadn't got into. Which was why I picked those, if you like, white songs for that set, because they had that dramatic content.' Of 'Phoenix . . .' he says, 'To preserve the vibe we cut it live, with no retakes – if you listen hard on the CD you can hear how my vocal mike picked up my fingernails clicking on the organ keys as I played those big swirls. When I played the whole album back to company bigwigs they sat there in shock. I got worried and said, "Well?" After a while the promotions manager said: "That motherfucker is awesome. Won't nobody give it airplay, but that ain't even gonna matter."' He was right, as within three months the album had outsold every LP the company had on release, reaching the top of the soul, jazz and pop charts. By the end of 1970 the album was platinum.

Neal Hefti

Nelson Riddle might have been responsible for most of the *Batman* TV series' incidental music, but the theme itself was composed by Neal Hefti. It was later recorded and performed live by the Jam (sounding very strange in the 100 Club) and subsequently became an icon of sixties trash. Hefti spent his early years as an arranger for the likes of Woody Herman and Count Basie before working with the Voice, Frank Sinatra. He was finally drafted into the movies, writing themes for such things as *How to Murder Your Wife* and *The Odd Couple*. The monosyllabic *Batman* theme wasn't typical of Hefti's style, though he has been quoted as saying, 'I attacked everything I wrote as a piece of theatre.'

Above: *Barefoot In The Park* was Neal Hefti's most brazen attempt at schmaltz

Below: *Vertigo!* Hitchcock's 1958 black comedy, is stunningly realized, helped enormously by Jimmy Stewart and Kim Novak's OTT performances, a biting script, startling cinematography and Bernard Hermann's unnerving score. Don't look up!

classic

Neal Hefti
'The Odd Couple' (1.16)
Album: Television's Greatest hits Volume II (TeeVee Toons Inc.) 1986
Hefti's magisterial theme tune was first heard in the original 1967 film, while the best version hails from the spin-off TV series, which ran for five years from 1970.

Bernard Herrmann
A pedantic autocrat and uncompromising perfectionist who raised the craft of filmscoring to an art, Herrmann worked on over fifty movies, including *Citizen Kane, Psycho,* the

original (and best) *Cape Fear, North By Northwest* and *Vertigo*. His collaboration with Hitchcock produced some of his most enduring work (according to George Martin, Herrmann's string arrangements for the maverick director influenced the orchestral backing for the Beatles' 'Eleanor Rigby'), yet he is best remembered for his vivid and haunting arrangements for *Taxi Driver* (he died, aged sixty-four, just before its release). The soundtrack is intercut with snippets of Robert DeNiro's dangerously quixotic dialogue. In the *Independent* recently, Jah Wobble chose this as one of his favourite records: 'I think of the music only in terms of mood and feeling. There are lovely thick jazz chords, not sweet or pleasant, and it sounds like there's a lot of sevenths and ninths in there . . . but what matters is that it moves me. Listen to this and it sets you up for the day.'

The High Llamas

Nowadays the work of Brian Wilson can be heard in everything from Portishead and Stereolab to Blur, the Boo Radleys and Pulp, but of all the people who have tried to lose themselves in the warmth of the sun, those who perhaps come closest are the High Llamas. *Gideon Gaye* (Alpaca Records, 1994) is the sound of Sean O'Hagan, chief High Llama, painstakingly trying to finish Wilson's lost masterpiece, *Smile,* using vibes, Vox organs, banjos, muted horns, violins and flutes (on one song, 'Track Goes By', flautist Marcel Corientes plays a solo for fifteen minutes). 'With a little Steely Dan thrown in for good measure (notably the single "Checking In, Checking Out"), it was every Brainhead's wet dream,' wrote Barney Hoskyns in *Mojo*. 'Slow MOR arrangements full of shakers and flutes and vibraphones; sugary baa-baa-baa harmonies, startlingly lovely chord changes; strings sliding around in a manner that suggested mild chemical imbalance. Nothing quite like "The Fire Section" of "The Elements Suite", I grant you, but a sound close to the strange rustic-baroque world of "Cabinessence".' And it only cost £2,500 to record.

Take one Brian Wilson melody, add distance, some technological advancement, and simmer

Their 1996 follow-up, *Hawaii*, took the vibrato-less organs, Moog interludes and even the sub-Van Dyke Parks Americana a few steps nearer the ocean with songs such as 'Snapshot Pioneer', 'The Hokey Curator' and 'Rustic Vespa'. 'Imagine classic Bacharach writing, but with Mingus brass and a Mike Nesmith feel,' says ex-Microdisney leader O'Hagan. 'Listening to this swooning seventy-seven minutes is like having a marshmallow explode on your tongue,' wrote *The Idler* on the album's release. O'Hagan's blush-tinted view of the world (both past and present) is summed up by the words to the gorgeous title track of *Gideon Gaye*: 'In the harbour town, perfect sunsets, People keep their yachts close at hand, The carparks are full of the giddy and gay as the band slips away . . .'

Above: The British crooner Michael Holliday sounded so much like Bing Crosby that Bing could do nothing but endorse him, time and time again. 'Michael, he's a great guy . . . one of the best there's ever been . . . a man among men . . . a singer beyond compare . . .' etc

Michael Holliday
'The Folks Who Live On The Hill' (3.10)
Album: Mike (EMI) 1959
Born in Dublin but raised in Liverpool, Holliday was Britain's own Bing Crosby, possessing a rich, deep voice that worked best when it was wrapped around standards like this. So laid back he makes Val Doonican seem like Joey Ramone.

Infra-music
In the grand scheme of things, perhaps it isn't surprising that Devo embroiled themselves in the world of meta-MOR. Having deconstructed Jagger and Richard's 'Satisfaction' with such panache in 1978, they turned the devolutionary lens on themselves in 1987, releasing *E-Z Listening Disc,* pseudo-elevator music cover versions of their own songs. Mark Mothersbaugh, Devo's self-appointed leader, explained his devout love of muzak – what he calls infra-music – in Joseph Lanza's highly personal history of all things lounge, *Elevator Music (*St. Martin's Press, 1994): 'Muzak helped me shape my musical politics. When I heard muzak versions of the Beatles, the Byrds and Bob Dylan, my goal was to do the same to my own music before anyone else did. Our *E-Z Listening Disc* has an interesting history. We were writing muzak-style versions of our own songs before we even had our first album out. We did a movie called *In The Beginning Was The End: The Truth About Devolution* in about 1976. It won first place in the Ann Arbor film festival. We recorded a Beatles song by running it through a frequency analyzer. I ripped a couple of things off an easy-listening channel and put them through this instrument. It became this bizarre robotic version of muzak-type songs. We were mutating muzak! When we first started performing, we wanted to have something like "An Evening With Devo", so we did our own muzak versions. Many people would come up to the soundman and ask to buy a tape [so] we recorded some for our fan club. Rock and roll is so bankrupt that, out of desperation, they'll [soon] be mining those territories.'

Jacky
'White Horses' (2.07)
Single (Philips) 1968
Childhood memories are incomplete without this piece of wet-behind-the-ears Arcadian kitsch, the signature tune of the rather twee sixties TV show.

Japan

Ten years ago, Japan was still as exotic as a distant planet, an unfathomable conundrum daring you to crack its extraordinary codes. Ten years ago, Tokyo didn't seem that much different from the dark, neon-lit city in Ridley Scott's sci-fi parable *Blade Runner* (well, apart from the flying machines and the androids, that is), its vast, futuristic landscape dwarfing and bewildering any stray Westerner who wandered into it. There was the architecture, the *Metropolis*-like elevated walkways, the street furniture, the automobiles, the public-service vehicles, the clothes, plus the dazzling array of electronic gadgets: the pocket fax machine, the laughing watch, the dancing robot, the Filofax that talked back; you name it, the Japanese produced it. If you wanted a little vending machine that offered the soiled undergarments of pre-pubescent schoolgirls, then you only had to come to Tokyo to find it. A vortex of demonstrative technology, it was as baffling as it was fascinating.

But the world has got a lot smaller in the last decade, and Tokyo these days is not so alien; in fact it doesn't look that different from midtown Manhattan. It is a mystery no longer; as the West has soaked up Japanese technology, and as Japan has embraced Western imagery and culture, so the two worlds seem bent on collision. Tokyo is awash with British and American pop culture, and everywhere you look you can find designer clothes, toys, books, videos and even fanzines imported from New York's Lower East Side and London's Camden Town. And the Tokyo record shops are a true phenomenon, rivalling the corporate megastores in London, New York or Los Angeles not only in size, but specifically in content. Because of a combination of bizarre copyright laws and an almost desperate fascination for the more arcane and obscure delights of Western pop, those records which you thought were long consigned to the pedal-bin of memory are here in all their PoMo, CD-re-released glory. Tokyo is the place where lounge music went to die, and where space age folk rock is awaiting resurrection, the home of twenty-first Century bossa nova beat groups such as the Pizzicato Five, Bridge and Seagull Screaming Kiss Her Kiss Her. These new Japanese loungecore artists go straight to the heart of the periphery, recreating the kind of music which was almost forgotten about from the

Centre left: Worried that they might be given the muzak treatment, Devo got there first, and even tried recording some of their new-found 'easy' songs in a lift. While they were unashamedly arty (such an awful word), the band had a goofiness which made them pass it off. Q: Are We Not Men? A: We Are Loungecore

Bottom left: Jacky was one of the sixties' more extraordinary one-hit wonders

Above: Never Never Pop was identified by the journalists Simon Reynolds and Frank Owen as theoretical pop which starts with an idea and then goes looking for the talent to fulfil it. Examples: ABC, ZTT, Sigue Sigue Sputnik, the Pizzicato Five. Will manifesto-mongering ever go out of fashion?

Below: Q: When is a door not a door? A: When it's a Jarre. Having worked as the director of the Paris Theatre National Populaire, Maurice Jarre dived into the movies, eventually composing lush, romantic scores for *Lawrence Of Arabia* (1962), *Doctor Zhivago* (1965), *Ryan's Daughter* (1970) and *The Man Who Would Be King* (1975). A rival, somewhat, of Michel Legrand

Bottom: The difference between Bert and a bull? One's got the horns at the front and . . .

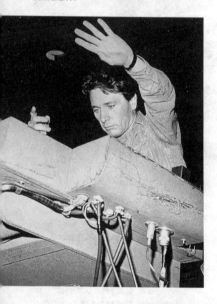

start – stuff made by Bas Sheva, the Bobby Hammack Combo, Sam Butera, the Guitars Unlimited Plus 7, Sid Bass, Synthesonic Sounds, John Cameron, the In Group, the City of Westminster String Band, Bob Peck, the Noveltones, the Bob Crewe Generation, Roger Nichols & the Small Circle of Friends, Blossom Dearie, Enoch Light, Tony Christie, Helena Vondrackova, etc.

The Pizzicato Five seem to be the sort of people who look at life through starburst filter contact lenses, while their quest for kitsch is unparalleled: with their 1996 LP *The Sound Of Music* (a blend of plastic dance-pop and Bacharach/Mendes spoofs), they gave away platinum 'Carte Pizzicato' credit cards – the type of ironic consumerist tat which can easily be found in any Japanese toy shop.

Japan became infatuated with lounge long before nightclub trendies in London or New York, with labels such as Trattoria committing themselves to building a library of outrageous space-age pop both old and new, and to graze the Trattoria landscape is to subject yourself to an aural safari through tropics of feverish rhythm and supple beats. Just when you thought you had had enough of eclecticism, along come a bunch of E-Z converts obsessed with the minutiae of loungecore pop, luxuriant mood music, winsome synthetic rock'n'roll, spy theme jazz, word jazz, South Sea Island sounds, kitsch instrumentals, cocktail tunes and the entrancing, borderless oceans of modern noise. Some have said that the premise for a lot of this music is nothing more than comfort, encapsulating a time 'when "revolution" meant watering down your scotch with ice, when "evolution" meant taking out the olive and putting in an onion'; in the hands of the Japanese it has become an art form.

Maurice Jarre

A three-time Oscar winner (*Lawrence Of Arabia,* 1962; *Doctor Zhivago,* 1965; *A Passage To India,* 1986), the Rick Wakeman of the movie soundtrack began his association with the cinema scoring the short films of Resnais and Franju. Predictably courted by Hollywood (*The Longest Day, Grand Prix, Fatal Attraction,* etc.), he is renowned for his restrained, 'sophisticated' arrangements. Still somewhat resented for siring Jean-Michel.

classic

Bert Kaempfert & His Orchestra
'A Swingin' Safari' (3.07)
Album: A Swingin' Safari (Polydor) 1962
Stabbing horns, penny whistles, silly strings and African rhythms – Kaempfert's music might seem perverse if it weren't so seductive.

Francis Lai

'Theme De Catherine' (2.50)

Album: Vivre Pour Vivre (United Artists) 1967

This extraordinary epiphany is typical of Lai's lush sixties French-movie themes. He also wrote frothy concoctions for *Love Is A Funny Thing*, *Love Story* and, er, *Emmanuelle*.

Francis Lai

'Un Homme Et Une Femme' (2.34)

Album: Un Homme Et Une Femme (United Artists) 1966

A soundtrack for the cocktail party of your dreams. The grand prize winner at the 1966 Cannes Film Festival, Claude Lelouch's piece of escapist schmaltz has one of the finest soundtracks of the decade. Since this came out, French country roads have never seemed the same, particularly the D106 to Vareche.

Duncan Lamont

'Desafinado' (2.16)

Album: The Best Of The Bossa Novas (MFP) 1970

Satin and tat, indeed. During the early seventies the Music For Pleasure label made a virtue out of so-so artists covering popular material. In the process, however, a lot of good, and sometimes great, records slipped through the net. This is one of the greats, a beautiful interpretation of Jobim's classic bossa nova. Other purveyors of cut-price, soon-to-be-remaindered, bargain-bin classics include the Hamlet, Pickwick, Hallmark and Marble Arch labels.

Liberace

Strange, yet true. Until his death in 1987, at the age of sixty-seven, Wladziu Valentine Liberace was one of the most fêted entertainers of the mid-twentieth century. He started in showbiz simply as a pianist, but, as Jane and Michael Stern have written, 'early in his career his substantial musical abilities were upstaged by the world's most flamboyant wardrobe, blinding batteries of jewellery, gilded pianos, and musical programmes of such stunning *mise-en-scène* they put the stars in heaven to shame'. Among Liberace's more infamous excesses were his forty-pound rhinestone jacket, the candelabras atop his pianos, his red, white and blue star-spangled Rolls-Royce (made for his extraordinary bicentennial

Top: Francis Lai: was there ever a more romantic orchestral arranger?

Centre: Duncan Lamont was the undisputed king of the bargain bin

Previous page: Liberace – with his dimpled grin, glass piano and knowing wink – was nothing if not an entertainer: his version of Chopin's 'Minute Waltz' lasted only thirty-seven seconds because he preferred to 'leave out the dull parts'

Top: Virna Lindt: even in the eighties the Cold War was raging somewhere

Bottom: Julie London appeared in the quintessential fifties film, *The Girl Can't Help It*

show at the Las Vegas Hilton), and the far-from-small toilet adjacent to the master bedroom in his Palm Springs home, remodelled to look like a royal throne. His most extreme acquisition was the face of his companion, Scott Thorson. In Thorson's book *Behind the Candelabra,* he recounts the story of Liberace asking a Beverly Hills plastic surgeon to restructure Thorson's face so it looked like a younger version of himself. When Liberace saw Thorson's new face for the first time, he stared at his Dorian Grey-like mirror-image and squealed, 'A beauty – a star is born.'

classic

Liberace
'Theme From A Summer Place' (2.25)
Album: The Best Of Liberace (MCA) 1972
Keyboards by candlelight! Melodramatic vamping at its best, with buckets of trills and double octaves. Compared to some of his material, this shows the spangly pianist in particularly restrained form.

classic

Virna Lindt
'Shiver' (2.53)
Album: Shiver (Compact) 1984
A cute spy-movie pastiche, all the way from Stockholm, via the murky backwaters of North London. Imagine Thomas Leer working with John Barry and you have this mondo exercise in musical subterfuge. An old grey trench coat will never let you down . . .

Julie London
The statuesque tragedienne is best remembered for her chillingly cold rendition of Arthur Hamilton's mournful, dolorous 1955 ballad, 'Cry Me A River'. Fashioned in dew and chiffon, she had a voice as brittle as glass, as soft as baby breath. Oh, girl.

Manhattan Tower
Cult records rarely live up to expectations, especially those which have become cyphers in the increasingly crowded world of kitsch'n'camp nostalgia. *Manhattan Tower,* however, is a real treasure. A paean to New York, this concept LP is a musical by Gordon Jenkins which charts the romance between two young city dwellers. Part narrated, part orchestrated, the ten songs on *Tower* are a guide to the Manhattan of the late forties/early fifties – 'music and romantic comedy; modern Americana full of the life and love and lore of a big city.'

'This love song to a city began in 1929 when Jenkins, an under employed musician, arrived in Gotham and was bewitched by the skyline, the people and the rich twenty-four-hour life. Sixteen years later he returned as a successful composer to work on *Manhattan Tower*. It was originally only twenty minutes long; the full forty-five-minute version was recorded in the fifties by Jenkins with his orchestra and the Ralph Brewster Singers for Capitol Records. Tremendously popular in its day, it's now almost impossible to find. It is worth the search, though, as Jenkins's homage is a towering achievement.

Manhattan Tower was an aural portrait of Gotham City in love

classic

Dean Martin

'You Belong To Me' (2.58)
EP: Relaxin' With Dean Martin (Capitol) 1954

More so than Sinatra, Crosby or Jack Jones, Dino – always cool, calm and collected – was a bona fide balladeer, a louche lounge lizard with a hang-dog expression and a seemingly unlimited supply of soft-centred love songs. Just like this.

Left: The one and only Dean Martin, the Jesus of Cool: 'Return To Me', 'The Naughty Lady Of Shady Lane', 'That's Amore', 'Volare', 'Under The Bridges Of Paris', 'You Belong To Me', 'Napoli', 'Gentle On My Mind', 'Ain't That A Kick In The Head', 'Pour Me A Pint Of Gin' etc

Near left: Somewhere it's always Mathis time: 'A Certain Smile', 'Misty', 'Wonderful! Wonderful!', 'The Twelfth Of Never', 'Come To Me', 'Wild Is The Wind', 'Evil Ways', 'Gina', 'What Will Mary Say', 'It's Too Late', 'Too Much, Too Little, Too Late', 'Friends In Love' etc

Johnny Mathis
'Wild Is The Wind' (2.25)
Album: Wild Is The Wind (Columbia) 1957
Made popular by David Bowie's overwrought 1976 version from his breathtaking *Station to Station* LP, the title theme of George Cukor's 1957 movie was written by Dimitri Tiomkin and originally recorded by 'the King of Necking Music'. A delightful interpretation, the record not only highlights Tiomkin's wandering-wondering melody, but it also showcases Mathis's sing-song vocal style. Though he is often considered a featherweight when compared with the likes of Sinatra, Bennett, Tormé and Dino, Mathis has had a remarkably varied and successful career; he even recorded a classic disco number 'Gone, Gone, Gone' on his 1979 LP *The Best Days of My Life*.

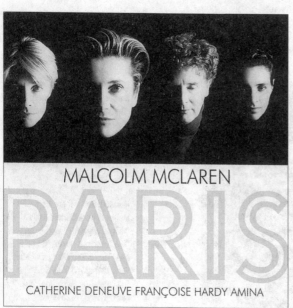

MALCOLM MCLAREN

PARIS

CATHERINE DENEUVE FRANÇOISE HARDY AMINA

'I wore black, You were black, Jazz is Paris, and Paris is Jazz'

Malcolm McLaren
'Jazz Is Paris' (5.12)
Album: Paris (Vogue) 1994
A Satie riff blown by a Miles Davis impostor, McLaren's preposterous homage to the French capital would be an insult if it weren't so funny. A kind of French *Absolute Beginners, Paris* is a typically eclectic grab-bag of the marvellous and the painfully self-conscious, a never-less-than-bizarre mix of musical styles which extol many of the clichéd virtues of Parisian café society. In a tribute to his adopted city, McLaren borrows melodies from Satie, eulogizes Davis, and incorporates the voices of the legendary chanteuse Françoise Hardy, Catherine Deneuve, and the French-Tunisian star Amina. Then there is the song inspired by Zola, the Senegalese drummers, the Serge Gainsbourg samples ('Gainsbourg was a huge Sid Vicious fan, you know,' says McLaren, 'used to keep a picture of him on his piano'), and of course McLaren's own particular *sprechgesang* (literally 'talk-singing'). 'This collection of songs attempts to inscribe a map of feelings over this jazz-drenched city, a city where I have often been lost in a daydream, listening to Satie, Art Blakey and Gainsbourg. Some of their blood and smells remain.' Gorgeous stuff from the Rachman of rock'n'roll, the Bill Sykes of *bricolage*.

classic

Sergio Mendes & Brasil '66

'Mas Que Nada' (2.39)
Single (A&M) 1966
One of the group's first hits, this sensational blend of bossa nova and jazz became a dancefloor favourite during the early eighties and an easy favourite in the nineties. Mendes has recorded dozens and dozens of Latin-lite classics, and no loungecore compilation is complete without him. Favourites include 'Never Can Say Goodbye', 'Fool On The Hill', 'Wave', Going Out Of My Head', and 'The Waters Of March', as well as 'Chelsea Morning', 'One Note Samba' and 'Scarborough Fair'. Mendes has been refreshingly catholic in his choice of material these past thirty years, though he has always managed to make any song he covers his own. At times his group (Brasil '65, '66, '77, '88, etc.) has included Dave Grusin and Lani Hall.

classic

George Michael

'Cowboys & Angels' (7.14)
Album: Listen Without Prejudice Vol. 1 (Epic) 1990
Not the most commercial of songs, but perhaps the little Greek God's finest hour (or at least seven minutes), a symphony in miniature to rival anything by Scott Walker, John Barry or Dionne Warwick. On his most recent LP, *Older,* Michael has pursued this penchant for soft, samba, cocktail rhythms; he even co-dedicated the album to Antonio Carlos Jobim, 'who changed the way I listened to music'. 'When your heart's in someone else's hands . . .'

classic

Joni Mitchell

'Edith & The King Pin' (3.35)
Album: The Hissing Of Summer Lawns (Asylum) 1976
When she put her mind to it, the Queen of El Lay could construct an arrangement that even Bacharach would have been proud of. This, from her best album, contains one of her loveliest melodies and bitterest lyrics.

Below: At his peak, Chris Montez covered everything that wasn't nailed down, using his extremely shrill voice on everything from 'The More I See You' and 'The Shadow Of Your Smile' to 'Call Me' and 'Time After Time'

Bottom left: A glass of wine, a cravat, and oodles and oodles of class

Bottom right: Matt Monro: 'We're Gonna Change Your World', 'Born Free', 'On Days Like These', 'Softly As I Leave You', 'From Russia With Love', 'And I Love Her', 'Portrait Of My Love', 'Yesterday', 'My Kind Of Girl', 'Walk Away', 'And You Smiled' etc

classic

Matt Monro
'On Days Like These' (3.33)
Album: The Very Best Of Matt Monro (MFP) 1974
The title song from the British 1969 caper movie *The Italian Job* (which also includes the riotous 'Self Preservation Society'), this is one of the most maudlin tracks Monro ever recorded. Incidentally, *The Italian Job* was the only film to star both Noel Coward and Benny Hill. Interesting.

classic

Chris Montez
'The More I See You' (2.45)
Single (Pye) 1966
Perhaps best known in Britain for his 1962 ballroom hit 'Let's Dance', Montez later made a virtue out of his castrato-style singing voice. This splendid Warren/Gordon confection is also included on Montez's 1975 fly-by-night LP *Time After Time*.

Moods In Music

George Melachrino's 'Moods In Music' LPs, recorded by the Melachrino Strings during the fifties, suggested that daily life could have a soundtrack, beginning with *Moods For Dining* ('Add that little bit of extra seasoning that turns an ordinary supper into an adventure,' whispered the sleeve notes) and continuing with *Music For Relaxation, Music For Reading, Music For Daydreaming* and even *Music For Courage And Inspiration.* Melachrino claimed, 'Now that modern science has come out in favour of it, everyone agrees on the good sense of listening to music while you are otherwise occupied.' Plans are afoot for some new recordings based on this theme: *Music For Drive-by Shootings, Music For Couch Potatoes* and *Music To Survive The Recession By* . . .

Alan Moorehouse

'Fool On The Hill' (2.53)
Album: Beatles, Bach & Bacharach Go Bossa (MFP) 1971
Honour thy error as a hidden intention. Moorehouse calls the arrangements of this and the other songs here ('Minuet In G', 'Do You Know The Way To San José', etc.) 'Happy Bossa', mixing flute, flugelhorn, tenor sax and electric harpsichord – a veritable soufflé of a disc.

Ennio Morricone

Bellisimo! The godfather of film music, Morricone is the man who put the opera into horse opera. He achieved fame with Sergio Leone's spaghetti Westerns (*A Fistful of Dollars, The Good, the Bad and the Ugly,* etc.), before going on to score over a hundred movies (including *The Mission* and *Cinema Paradiso*), and is among the most prolific and versatile composers in the business. Responsible for the monumental *Once Upon a Time in America,* which, even more so than his *Once Upon A Time in the West,* is probably the greatest film score ever recorded: a twentieth-century masterpiece.

Top: Anything, if one puts one's mind to it, can be set to the bossa-nova. Especially Bach

Bottom: Ennio Morricone brought a surrealistic panorama of strange cries, savage guitar chords, jangling bells and the cracking of whips to Sergio Leone's early westerns (once described as sounding like Mitch Miller on dope), and he hasn't looked back since

A glittering novelty or a macabre piece of fortune-telling, Terry Gilliam's 1985 extravaganza *Brazil* was blessed with an equally intricate and explosive soundtrack. What price success in the Ministry of Information? Go ask Jonathan Pryce

Geoff Muldaur

'Brazil' (3.28)

Album: Brazil (Milan) 1992

Included on the belated soundtrack LP of Terry Gilliam's 1985 extravaganza, Muldaur's manic version of Ary Barroso's 'Aquarela Do Brasil' is post modern in the extreme. A cameo as bizarre as De Niro's.

Muzak

by Tony Parsons

Background music is the junk mail of the ether. Unsolicited, it seeps into every nook and cranny of our lives. It oozes from the telephone when you are waiting to be connected. It percolates into lifts, lobbies, supermarkets, pubs and planes preparing for take-off. You can't stop the muzak.

The genre is known by many names. Piped music. Elevator music. Supermarket music. Aural Valium. The people who make it call it business music or programmed music – meaning music that is here not to be listened to, but to sell something. But most of all, this ubiquitous soundtrack is known as muzak.

But there is muzak and there is Muzak. There is the catch-all for background music and there is the Muzak Limited Partnership. Like Xerox, Hoover, Kleenex and Biro, Muzak is a brand name that has become a generic.

AEI-Rediffusion Music, the American-owned company which dominates background music in Britain, understandably avoids the word. 'Muzak is now a pejorative term,' says Chris Ring, AEI's managing director. 'People say to us, oh you do muzak. And we say, well, Muzak is a brand name actually – we do programmed music, business music.'

The case against background music is that it's insipid and anaemic – a bit like a Phil Collins record wih Phil Collins taken out. When we think of background music we think of interminable tinkly instrumentals and substandard cover versions. That was true ten years age. But not today.

You can still hear plenty of light instrumentals that make James Last sound like Led Zeppelin. But the great leap forward has been the increased use of music by original artists. In America ninty-five per cent of AEI clients buy original recordings. In Britain, where licensing charges are twice as high, just under half of AEI's clients use originals. This is background music for the generations who have been raised on rock music – that is, practically everyone under the age of fifty. AEI's Revolution CDi 'jukebox' contains a single, Japanese-designed compact disc that plays for more than ten hours. The names on the one I saw included Elvis, Bowie, Hendrix, the Jam, Wilson Pickett, the Doors, Cream – hardly the insipid muzak of popular myth.

'Costs increase dramatically using original artists,' says Chris Ring. 'You have to pay a fee to Phonographic Performance Ltd, which collects for the record companies, as well as organizations like the Performing Right Society and the Mechanical Copyright Protection Society, which collects for the publishers. But it's a price that a generation who grew up on pop is often prepared to pay.'

Ring's background was in marketing. 'I was Fred the Flour Grader at Home Pride,' he boasts, and he launched Red Mountain coffee – but his

Chill out! Muzak's music travels from its Seattle headquarters via satellite to receivers in 200,000 businesses across America. Each site has its own receiving code so that Muzak's twelve channels can be geared to a specific audience, ethnic community, geographical area – even the time of day

great passion is music. 'I love Tori Amos, Richard Thompson, Todd Rundgren, Mary Chapin Carpenter and Nancy Griffiths. I buy a lot of old stuff on CD.'

Ring – a boyish forty-year-old – is part of the generation which grew up with music as the lodestone to life, but says he does not want music everywhere. 'I don't want it in a park.' But like many people who were children during Beatlemania, he believes it should be everywhere else.

At AEI in Orpington, Kent, young men with rock'n'roll haircuts and the odd discreet earring trawl diligently through the backwaters of pop's history to find music for every location. Surrounded by small mountains of CDs in a warren of mixing studios, they seek a suitably mellow Marvin Gaye track here, a mellifluous Jethro Tull track there, fine tuning their tapes to fit an infinite variety of business needs.

Whistle While You Work has become 'Wire the World' (the battle cry of AEI president Mike Mallone).

The Muzak company has moved away from tape and CD. Muzak's music travels from its Seattle headquarters via satellite to receivers in 200,000 businesses across America. Each site has its own receiving code so that Muzak's twelve channels can be geared to a specific audience, ethnic community, geographic area – even the time of day.

Likewise, AEI has labyrinthine demographic strategies. In Orpington there is a tape library containing 26,000 titles, supplying 15,000 clients with seventeen music styles (including Timeless Pop, Nostalgia, Urban Contemporary, Espanol and Ethnic . . .) at five different energy levels (Mild, Easy, Medium, Up and Hot).

Are you a Mature Baby Boomer? An Energetic Retiree? A Suburban Student? A Metro Sophisticate? An Active Female? They have something for everyone. Background music does not want to annoy you. Background music wants to be your *friend*.

'We see ourselves as environmental designers,' says Chris Ring. 'Classical music or hip-hop music are going to make very different statements. A Burger King will play fairly fast music because it wants people to eat up and go. But an upmarket restaurant wants to slow them down, so they have the coffee and the extra sweet.'

The background music industry is awash with buzzwords, corporate philosophies and theories. There is talk of 'lifestyle marketing' (music that makes an image statement) and 'stimulus progression' (music that plots the fatigue cycles of a working day, picking up the tempo just when worker's droop sets in).

But in Adrian Pennink's brilliant Channel 4 documentary, *Beautiful Music*, Prof James J. Keenan of America's Fairfield University – and a psychologist consulted by Muzak – said that background music's *raison d'être* was very simple. It is there because most people like it. 'People like

Easy Discs

Everything happened in 1966, including Quincy Jones's haunting score for Sidney Lumet's Euro-thriller, *The Deadly Affair*, starring James Mason and Simone Signoret. Astrud Gilberto guests on the main title

Kaempfert was the man who inadvertently introduced the Beatles to Tommy Sheridan, which led to the group's first studio recordings. Kaempfert himself developed a unique style, sometimes called supermarket swing

If, as Umberto Eco wrote, 'Disneyland tells us that technology can give us more reality than nature can', then what on earth are we to make of little Gunter Kallman?

Just an old-fashioned girl exploiting old-fashioned fears of the exotic femme fatale. Her peers liked cocktails, diamonds and clutch-bags full of married men

Easy Discs

Lai's quintessential scores for *A Man And A Woman* combined piano, harpsichord, strings, electric bass, pop percussion and 'a constant yet bewitching volley of Gregorian cocktail la-la-las'. Ooh la la!

Beginning as a songwriter for Yves Montand and Edith Piaf, Francis Lai found a home in the movies, creating a fascinating dream-world of unrequited love set to evocative soundscapes

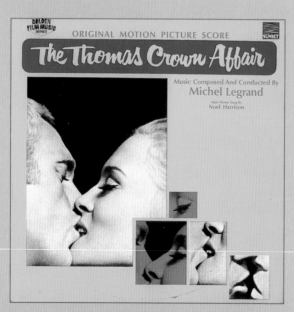

Though responsible for 'What Are You Doing The Rest Of Your Life?', 'Summer Of '42' and the John Barry homage 'The Go-Between', this remains Legrand's finest hour (or so)

'I wanted a classic string sound,' said the Niagara Falls of fiddles, the gush of lush. 'I wanted an overlapping sound, as though we were playing in an extremely large cathedral'

Easy Discs

A man of legendary singularity, Dino single-handedly invented cool. He was the epitome of louche sangfroid – a singer, actor and star who conquered Hollywood, television and Tin Pan Alley. Respect

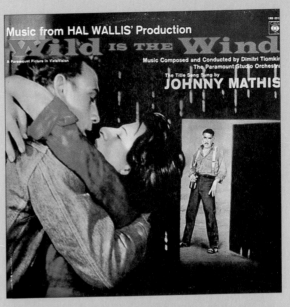

Johnny Mathis gave his songs an immediate and enduring poignancy, His *Greatest Hits* – released in 1958, a year after *Wild Is The Wind* - stayed on the Billboard charts for over ten years

He invented Euro bossa-nova, and with it a palpable example of Jet Set culture. Sergio Mendes not only transformed mainstream Brazilian tunes, he also jazzed-up (literally) pop classics

You'll believe a man can fly? You'll believe a man can sing like a girl? Take Chris Montez, a man with the strangest voice this side of Pee-Wee Herman. Or Tiny Tim, come to that

Easy Discs

WILD STRINGS
Werner Müller and his Orchestra

Did Werner Muller *really* get it? After all, you can change your perception as much as you like, but until you change the content of your perception, nothing changes at all

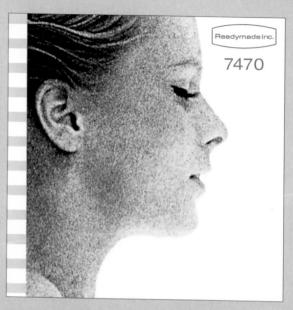

Readymade Inc.

7470

Dedicated to championing the best of the forgotten past, the Tokyo-based Readymade Hall of Fame is a lending library of the absurd, the obtuse and the sublime. Checking in or checking out?

Sea of Dreams
NELSON RIDDLE

Designing elegant scenery for the likes of Sinatra and Nat 'King' Cole, New Jersey-born Nelson Riddle wrote for the movies, for television, and recorded dozens of his own albums

The Sandpipers
Guantanamera

Aimed at an intergenerational audience, the Los Angeles-based vocal trio followed 'Guantanamera' (1966) with – Hold It, Tonto! – the theme from Russ Meyer's *Beyond The Valley Of the Dolls*. Way to go!

Easy Discs

Frank fact. Bill Zehme: 'How do you know when you've picked the right barber?' Frank Sinatra: 'When you leave the shop and no one hands you a hat, you're okay'

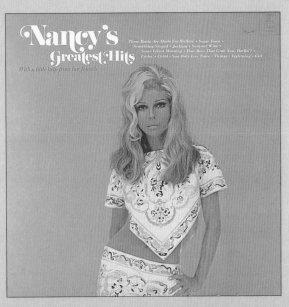

Nancy with the laughing face, a fox of the first order, and a famous sibling to boot. Iconic, ironic and unashamedly erotic, images like this (1970) will last forever. On your knees

She was called 'the legendary Sun Virgin', whilst her albums came with tongue-in-cheek disclaimers: 'When you play this, prepare for a long, strange voyage into a new land of sound'

The Swingle Singers were formed in 1962 by Fulbright scholar, pianist, singer and arranger Ward Lamar Swingle, with the original intention of vocalizing big-band instrumentals. But Baroque soon bit

Easy Discs

Recorded in September 1966, *Place Vendôme* was an unqualified success, a unique mixture of abstract jazz devices and sweet vocal harmonies, the Swingles interpreting songs by MJQ leader John Lewis

The blueprint for many a lounge lizard, Swing Out Sister were mixing Northern Soul with Bacharach and Jimmy Webb when the world was still dancing to Living In A Box and Johnny Hates Jazz

These days nostalgia knows no bounds, creating a market for everything from movie scores to advertising jingles, and any TV theme from *The Flintstones* to *Vegas*

Before long-distance travel became a birthright for baby-boomer Americans, Europe was more exotic than Hawaii, Cuba or the Florida Keys. So people learned to travel at home

Easy Discs

Hardly the master of love balladry, Scott Engel's bleak, elliptical solo work gave him a profile – obstinate, dour – similar to that of his hero, the enigmatic Jacques Brel

It's strange, but in a shrunken world in which few things still seem remote or exotic, Brazil retains its status as a haven of heavenly (and alliterative) hedonism. Will you fly down to Rio?

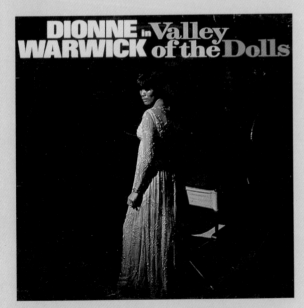

The ultimate sixties buppie icon, Dionne Warwick(e) grew up in a family soaked in gospel, performed at the Apollo and toured with her aunt Cissy Houston before turning pop into gold

They don't make records like this any more, so clearly we don't deserve them. America's greatest black female singer, its greatest living composer, and its finest interpreter of Jimmy Webb songs

Easy Discs

A cabaret star of the forties, a minor rock'n'roller in the fifties, Andy Williams found true fame when television allowed him to display his relaxed singing style and smooth 'fireside' personality

Sing! Cafe-au-lait smooth, Danny Williams was a hawk-eyed croonster, able to spot a decent ballad at considerably more than twenty paces. A top man, no less

How acute is the German sense of irony? Judging by a recent spate of exquisite compilations and re-releases it is far sharper than many might have imagined, or, indeed, expected

Travel report: It doesn't matter what it might be (how strange, or how arcane), these days if you want it, you've only got to go to a Japanese record store to find it. Soft rock rocks!

music rather than no music,' he said. 'They don't even know that they hear it sometimes. But they like it anyhow.'

Not all of them. A group called Pipe Down, which campaigns against piped music, makes it sound rather like a hole in the ozone layer around society's soul. The organization, which counts Spike Milligan and George Melly among its members, says, 'Too much unwanted noise is a health threat. It's known to raise blood pressure, increase stress and lower the immune system.'

The composer Sir Peter Maxwell Davies recently called for the cessation of all background music. 'You go to a restaurant,' he wrote. 'There is a racket going on. You cannot concentrate on a conversation at all. Half of you is engaged in blocking out the dreadful tape it is playing. It is supposed to make our environment friendlier, more helpful, more relaxing. Instead it dulls our senses and drives us mad.'

Ted Nugent, the heavy metal rock musician, once bid $10 million for Muzak just so that he could have the pleasure of wiping all its tapes. 'If anything is actually designed for the background then get it out of here,' he roared. 'Foreground – that's the name of life.'

The companies which actually use background music deny that it drives their customers insane. They see it is a good thing that makes their businesses more user-friendly.

Wilkinson's, a fast-growing home, leisure and garden chain in the North and Midlands, plays sixties music. 'Everything from the Beatles, Stones and Monkees to Des O'Connor,' says Paul Wilkinson. 'We actually have customers asking where they can buy the tapes. It creates a fun atmosphere and it lets people know we care.'

Adams, the children's-wear chain, is planning to raise the profile of its background music. The firm's 302 stores are moving from a bland wash of non-copyright music – the kind of stuff that you and I recognize as muzak – to something more funky.

'Muzak turns people off,' says Brian Smith, the company's retail operations director. 'In the past the music we used was actually *designed* to be bland. And as background music actually costs quite a lot to install and run, we are looking to make more use of it.'

Aren't they taking a risk by making the music more noticeable? 'We don't want to drive anyone out of our stores,' says Adams. 'Our marketing department will compile a detailed profile of the Adams customer. Age, musical tastes, everything. We will give that information to AEI-Rediffusion and they will come up with the music. Then we will test it in a few stores.'

And what does Adams get out of it?

'Simply that our customers feel more comfortable in our stores,' says Brian Smith. 'Music is a marketing tool. We believe that we haven't used it to its full potential in the past.'

Prof Roderick Swanston, head of undergraduate academic studies at the Royal College of Music insists that background music has always been with us. 'One of the most provocative composers who deliberately produced background music was Erik Satie. He hated pretentiousness.

'He once went up to Debussy, who was taking his music very seriously when conducting *La Mer*. The first movement of *La Mer* is a picture of the sea from dawn to midday and Satie said, "Claude, this is a wonderful piece. I especially like the little passage at a quarter to eleven."'

Bach's *Goldberg* Variations were written for an insomniac German count, says Prof Swanston. A divertimento was very often to accompany wedding guests chatting during a celebration. And in the late nineteenth century, Satie devised what he called amenity music.

'Satie engaged some musicians for the opening of a department store and their job was to be a kind of musical furniture – to be part of the background, the ambience,' says Prof Swanston. 'But as soon as the music started, people stopped and listened and clapped at the end. Satie got on to the platform and said to them, "Keep talking, keep talking! I don't want you to listen to my music."'

That's the trouble with background music – it can be so intrusive. The anti-muzak dissidents of Pipe Down refuse to acknowledge that there is even the remotest connection between a divertimento and what they are playing in the Woolwich.

'There is a hell of a difference between ceremonial or festive music, which is occasional and fairly rare, and having this stuff constantly drumming into you all the time,' says a spokesman. 'To give a comparison – if you went to a cinema or a theatre which you had chosen and suddenly someone rushed up and began feeding you a meal. It might be a good meal, it might be a horrible meal – but you haven't chosen that meal and you may not feel at all hungry. And that's the sort of thing that piped music does – it's forcing people to listen to it.'

Prof Swanston agrees that there is a point where background music starts to tamper with our emotions. But doesn't a Mozart piano sonata manipulate us just as much as the AEI tapes with names like 'Smooth Sounds', 'Gentle Sounds' and 'Sounds Sentimental'?

A Gallup poll suggested that eighty-six percent of customers thought music improved the atmosphere in a shop – then why is it so hard to find anyone to stand up for it? And does it work?

'It's very, very difficult to prove that people spend more money as a result of having music there,' says Ring. 'I wouldn't claim that they do. Surveys have been done that say it does, surveys have been done that say it doesn't. But ultimately I think we make business run more smoothly and make the world a better place. There has always been background music. We are just doing it better now.'

Background music is an imprecise science. Its major PR problem is that when it is working well, you don't know it is there. But more music designed for the *foreground* is now becoming part of the scenery. In every shopping mall and on every street, the volume is being turned up as rock, dance and reggae – music very much made to be listened to – all bellow in the background.

The world is getting louder. And the real danger is that some time very soon, all music will be background music.

(First published in the *Daily Telegraph*, 1994.)

Anthony Newley

'Goldfinger' (2.49)
Album: The Best Of James Bond (30th Anniversary Limited Edition) (United Artists) 1992
Not released until nearly thirty years after it was recorded, this supremely arch version of the Bricusse/Newley/Barry classic was considered too camp for inclusion in the movie, so the producers opted for the more strident Shirley Bassey. Did anyone order mince?

One From The Heart

Francis Coppola's magnificent failure produced a soundtrack of enduring passion and ennui. The inspired pairing of Tom Waits and Crystal Gayle in songs like 'Old Boyfriends' and 'Take Me Home' (like everything else here, written by Waits) creates such a sense of sugar-coated melancholy that you don't know whether to laugh or cry. The songs are lent even more poignancy because of the subterranean backdrop against which Coppola uses them – a somnambulent suburbia on the edges of a virtual Las Vegas, an environment entirely composed of margins.

Perrey & Kingsley

Years before Kraftwerk or Giorgio Moroder, Jean-Jacques Perrey and Gershon Kingsley were experimenting with the physical and emotional possibilities of electronic music: 'robots with soul' they called their machines. United by a firm conviction that Moog and synthesizers need not – and should not – be cold, forbidding and strange, during the sixties and seventies they not only recorded their own bizarre compositions, but also covered standards like 'Strangers In The Night', 'Moon River', 'Lover's Concerto' and 'One Note Samba', creating a new musical genre in the process.

Top: It was not, obviously, a panther, but rather a diamond, sought in the original 1963 movie, by suave thief David Niven. Though it reappeared in 1974's *The Return Of The Pink Panther,* it was symptomatically forgotten in subsequent efforts

Above: Do you still wanna get loaded? Having been somewhat left behind by the whole Britpop thing, Primal Scream seem destined to turn into a hotel-trashing, prescribed-drug indulging, groupie-happy-type rock'n'roll band. But they don't seem to be too worried about it

Right: Known as 'El Ray del Mambo', Perez Prado was largely responsible for the popularity of the Mambo in North America in the fifties and had two of the decade's most successful records, 'Cherry Pink & Apple Blossom White' (1955) and 'Patricia' (1958). An enduring star in South America, he toured there until he moved to Italy in the early seventies

The Pink Panther

Der dum, der dum . . . Henry Mancini's low-down themes for the series *Peter Gunn* and *Mr Lucky* were hailed as the first modern jazz scores on TV, although in fact they were closer to Hollywood. Which is where he ended up, writing 'Moon River' and hordes of film scores, notably Orson Welles's *A Touch of Evil, Days of Wine and Roses,* and, of course, the omnipresent Pink Panther theme. Rinky dink.

Perez Prado

The Mambo King, Prado was responsible for dozens of excitable Latin hits, including 'Patricia', 'Cherry Pink And Apple Blossom White', 'Why Wait' and 'Guaglione', which was successfully used in an ad campaign by Guinness in 1994. A big influence on Xavier Cugat, Prado played around with tone-poems, percussive horns, amplified grunts, and was one of the first to use the organ in pop music as a predominant instrument. Classic albums include *Voodoo Suite* and *Havana 3a.m.* (recorded in 1956 during the Batista era). Mam-boooo!

classic

Primal Scream

'Inner Flight' (5.02)
Album: Screamadelica (Creation) 1991
Bobby Gillespie's almost quaint homage to *Smile*-era Beach Boys. Drugs? No one mentioned drugs, did they?

classic

Nelson Riddle

'Lolita Ya Ya' (3.20)
Album: Lolita (MCA) 1961
The jaunty and rather barmy refrain from the soundtrack to Kubrick's noir comedy. So sixties it hurts.

classic

Rogue

'Somewhere Down The Line' (3.48)
Album: Would You Let Your Daughter . . . (Ariola) 1979
Written by Guy Fletcher and Douglas Flett, this beautiful torch song deserves to be resurrected, and is crying out to be covered by the likes of Michael McDonald or Celine Dion.

Below: Songs by Guy Fletcher and Douglas Flett, cover by David Bailey

Top right: From the opening shot showing a helicopter lifting a statue of Christ into the skies and out of Rome, Fellini's 1960 masterpiece *La Dolce Vita* develops into a Godless foray into wanton abandonment, peopled by Marcello Mastroianni and Anita Ekberg and underpinned by Nino Rota's petulant score

Bottom right: The original and – too, too obviously – the best big-screen version of *Lolita*, Stanley Kubrick's 1961 adaptation of the Nabokov novel stars James Mason as the repressed paedophile Humbert Humbert, Peter Sellers in the role of Quilty, and Nelson Riddle's never-less-than eccentric score. 'Ya-ya, ya-ya, ya-ya . . .'

Nino Rota

The late, great Milanese composer worked for over a quarter of a century with Fellini (*La Strada, La Dolce Vita, Satyricon, Roma,* etc.) before joining Francis Coppola for the first two (let's face it, the *only* two) *Godfather* films, winning an Academy Award for the sequel in 1974. Also composed four symphonies, eight operas, several concertos, ballet scores and numerous orchestral works. No slouch, he.

The Sandpipers

Discovered by A&M chief Herb Alpert in 1965 when they were still the Grads, Mike Piano, Jim Brady and Richard Shoff shot to stardom when they recorded an elaborate vocal version of a Cuban folk song called 'Guantanamera' which they had first heard on a Pete Seeger disc recorded live at Carnegie Hall. Once described by the former Beatles publicist Derek Taylor as 'the squarest group in the world; boy were they STRAIGHT, a dull bunch of ex-Mitchell Boy choristers'. Asked by the band to overhaul their image (scarves and moustaches were what they had in mind), Taylor rather belligerently declined, advising them instead to start dropping acid.

The Sandpipers' staggering version of 'Never Can Say Goodbye' (which has now become a soul property) is one of life's little luxuries, not to be indulged too often, lest one becomes addicted

classic

Santos & Johnny

'Sleepwalk' (2.23)
Album: Mermaids Soundtrack (Epic) 1990
A remarkably twangy guitar surf standard which manages to bring most of the more spectacular parts of Hawaii into your front room in a little over two minutes. The Chantays had nothing on Santos & Johnny.

Sing Something Simple

In 1959, the BBC asked Cliff Adams to present a new programme featuring his band of singers – a programme based on the premise that people never tire of the nostalgic and the evocative. So successful was the formula that, thirty-six years later, the show is still running, and is as much a part of the culture of Radio 2 as the dulcet tones of David Jacobs or Jimmy Young.

Right: Surf music has always been an extremely broad church, encompassing everything from heads-down, see-you-at-the-end instrumentals, Beach Boys-style teen epiphanies, barbecue duets (in particular see Guy Paellert and Nik Cohn's *Rock Dreams*), plus the occasional twang-heavy ballad, like 'Sleepwalk' by Santos & Johnny. Dive in, why don't you, the water's lovely

Below: It was a different world, the old world: quaint, polite and rather stuck in its ways. There were regimes, too: 7pm, Sunday, as the wind-down from the weekend kicked in. How could you not Sing Something Simple?

Soundtracks

Whitney Houston's pop promos look like toothpaste commercials at the best of times, so no one should have been surprised when she turned in a particularly anodyne performance in *The Bodyguard*. She obviously borrowed her acting style (if, indeed, that's what it is) from Roger Moore, from whom she has learned to raise and wriggle her eyebrows to great effect.

But the reason the movie was such a monstrous success had nothing to do with the novelty of seeing Whitney on screen; nor can Kevin Costner's haircut (idiosyncratic, receding, combed forward) take the credit; nor the sex (there wasn't any to speak of). No, the reason that half the Western world (and not necessarily the educated half) flocked to see *The Bodyguard* was to hear Whitney sing That Song.

Because of the inclusion of 'I Will Always Love You', *The Bodyguard* soundtrack stayed at the top of the Billboard charts for over six months, the most successful movie tie-in for a decade. The movie itself – which is nothing more than an extended promo for the song – took well over $100 million in North America alone. Symbiosis is the name of the game, which is one of the reasons why They Don't Make 'Em Like They Used To. Movie soundtracks, that is.

The golden age of the Hollywood soundtrack coincided with the golden age of the Hollywood musical, when Richard Rodgers, Lorenz Hart, Oscar Hammerstein, Frederick Loewe, Alan Jay Lerner, George and Ira Gershwin, Leonard Bernstein, Cole Porter and Irving Berlin each carved themselves a little bit of history. From the early thirties to the mid sixties, the American musical was more or less in charge of its own destiny, commanding respect and attention from the studios, the critics and the public alike. It died, as all things must, during the sixties, when the musical suddenly seemed so anachronistic, woefully at odds with a culture quickly acclimatizing to Vietnam, teenage insurrection, the Beatles, TV, and dope.

Consequently the soundtrack relinquished its pole position in the Hollywood hierarchy and took on a more subservient role. By its very nature, the soundtrack is a supplementary medium, in much the same way as the video promo. It's intrusive and indistinct by turns, following the film like a shadow. A soundtrack is like a reliable minder: there when you need it. 'The most important thing for movie writing is the atmosphere, the spirit, the uplift,' says John Barry. 'Being accurate to a scene – hitting that scene's feelings accurately and giving it the sense of tragedy, joy, whatever it is. That's the fun of it. I adore music, but when I'm sitting there watching . . . *that's* the boss. The picture is God. Music is secondary.'

Having said that, it's almost impossible to imagine the shower scene in

Psycho without Bernard Herrmann's stabbing violins, or the shark in *Jaws* without John Williams's rampaging bass lines. Similarly it's difficult to think of the opening sequence to *Manhattan* without 'Rhapsody In Blue' swamping the skyline; hard to see Rocky Balboa running through the streets of Philadelphia without the TV cop-show strains of the Rocky Theme ('Gonna Fly Now') pumping through the aisles.

Would *Brief Encounter* have made such an impact without the help of Rachmaninov's Second Piano Concerto? Could *Easy Rider* have date-stamped the *zeitgeist* without Steppenwolf's 'Born To Be Wild'? Can you imagine Louis Malle's *Ascenseur Pour L'Echafaud* without the Miles Davis score? Like classic pop, movie music defines the age, creating nostalgia right before our eyes. It is *our* music, reminding us not only of the movie it came with, but also of what we were doing at the time, how we felt, and who we were with when we saw it. The best soundtracks offer exhilaration, pathos, anger, and sentiment; while the really good ones remind us that there is a redemptive quality lurking somewhere in the darkness. Film music is the glue that holds the mass together, a velvet wrap for our dreams.

Can movie soundtracks ever be this good again? Go ask John Barry

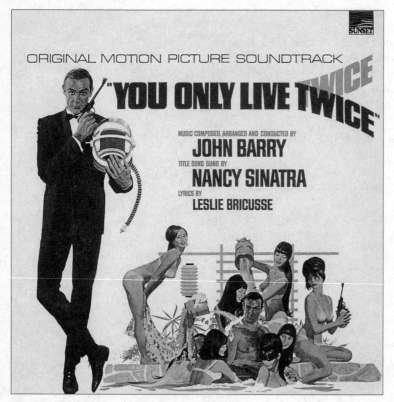

If, like Donald Fagen says, good music should sabotage expectations, then there is very little good music in the movies. Aural clichés are as widespread as visual ones: jazz for the city, narcissistic flutes in the suburbs; Aaron Copeland-style orchestration for small-town Americana; scratchy guitars and piping horns for urban thrillers. For pastoral, copy Debussy; for devastation, rework Barber or Albinoni; for a Western, hire Morricone.

Cinema has, however, thrown up some legendary composers: John Barry, Neal Hefti, Bernard Herrmann, Maurice Jarre, Francis Lai, Nino Rota, Ennio Morricone, Max Steiner, Dimitri Tiomkin, Lalo Schifrin, Jerry Goldsmith, Jack Nitzsche, Michael Nyman, Gabriel Yared and John Williams are all men who have made music to watch, men who have conjured up something special from the dark. Today's stars include Danny Elfman (*Beetlejuice, Dick Tracy,* etc.), whose foreboding themes made Tim Burton's *Batman* almost bearable; Alan Silvestri, who wrapped sound around *Who Framed Roger Rabbit, The Abyss* and the *Back to the Future* films; and Angelo Badalamenti, whose infectious hymns for David Lynch's *Twin Peaks* will surely last longer than either the series or the movie.

Saturday Night Fever was the first film to forge a symbiotic relationship between movies and music, a relationship which now determines that both media hype each other contemporaneously. 'The difference between pre-*Saturday Night Fever* and post-*Saturday Night Fever,*' says Gary LeMel, president of music at Warner Bros, 'is that before, songs from movies would sometimes be hits because people would love the movie, love the song, and maybe buy the record after seeing the movie. Before that, nobody used music as a tool to premarket a film in the way *Fever* did and the way everybody does now.'

There's much to enjoy but little to admire about modern-day Hollywood. The eighties bred the type of soundtracks which complemented the type of movies in which actors talked in bumper stickers. Mainstream Hollywood movies became multi-media events, force-fed packages to be consumed at once, rather than at will: *Flashdance, Footloose, Back to the Future, Pretty in Pink, The Breakfast Club,* ad nauseam. Soundtracks have been hijacked by record companies, as orchestrated scores become marginalized by collections of songs that are specially recorded for the film; either that or collections of oldies (*American Graffiti, Diner, The Big Chill)* or combinations of the two (*Mermaids, Dirty Dancing).*

When Cubby Broccoli's successor decides to film the next Bond movie, he could do worse than put John Barry together with Whitney Houston. Anything would be better than dear old Tina Turner.

Space-age Pop
by Irwin Chusid

Space-age pop is back. After its heyday in the late fifties and early sixties, these imaginative instrumental stylings fell from fashion, were forgotten, skipped a generation or two, then re-emerged as a fresh source of sonic balm in the nineties.

The tag 'space-age pop' is generic, yet broad. Along with such RCA recording artists as Henry Mancini, Ray Martin, and Bernie Green, the field encompasses the lounge organ mastery of Lenny Dee; the

107

Polynesian sway of Martin Denny and Les Baxter; the cinematic colourings of Nino Rota; the 1,001-string magnificence of Mantovani; and the prepared piano novelties of Ferrante and Teicher.

Space-age pop frames a period, roughly 1954 to 1964 – from the dawn of high-fidelity (hi-fi) to the arrival of the Beatles. At its inception, hi-fi (and subsequently stereo) technology provided record companies with a showcase for the pan-galactic spectrum of audio reproduction. Artists like Esquivel, Enoch Light and Sauter-Finegan led the way in showing off their studio smarts. A decade later, the British Invasion, accompanied by Dylanesque cultural and political upheaval, altered popular music forever; the most renowned instrumental pop artists changed their courses correspondingly, or disappeared from vinyl.

Space-age pop pre-dates popular acceptance of the electronic sound generation. For the most part, these recordings were made with conventional acoustic and electric instruments. There's an occasional theremin or ondioline, but no synthesizers. Classic space-age pop even pre-dates the Moog. The state-of-the-art studio toolkit included tape speed manipulation, multi-tracking, controlled distortion, reverb, equalization and tape editing (with razor blades). Conductors assumed the roles of magicians; engineers became alchemists. Despite similarities in big band instrumentation, these recordings were light years from Glenn Miller.

It should be pointed out that the phrase space-age pop wasn't in vogue when this music was created. That term arose during the mid-eighties, when cultural trash-pickers were scavenging through thrift store bins and used-record shops, paying 50 cents an armload for the stuff – because nobody else wanted it. Moreover, the vinyl archaeologists who bought those cast-off relics developed a new (or in some cases renewed) appreciation for the quirky signals etched in the grooves. I credit Los Angeles artist Byron Werner with coining the phrase 'space-age bachelor pad music' – later shortened to space-age pop by myself.

This music was popular when it was originally released. It was a great way to test the capabilities of a new stereo – or the limits of your neighbour's patience. But after a decade of glory, the novelty wore off and the music became outdated, superseded by higher-tech hijinks and countercultural weirdness. A zillion trends have come and gone – mostly gone – since. There was bound to be a time when the cocktail-glass tintinnabulations of Bob Thompson or the springy rhythms of the Three Suns would become fashionable again.

That day has arrived.

Though many band leaders (such as Henri René and Bob Thompson) composed, most relied on radical reworkings of Tin Pan Alley standards, or borrowings from the classical repertoire. Juan Garcia Esquivel, asked

Space-age pop frames a period, roughly 1954 to 1964 - from the dawn of high-fidelity (hi-fi) to the arrival of the Beatles. At its inception, hi-fi (and subsequently stereo) technology provided record companies with a showcase for the pan-galactic spectrum of audio reproduction. Artists like Esquivel, Enoch Light, and Sauter-Finegan led the way here

why he often used such familiar material for his eccentric orchestrations, explained, 'When a listener hears a song he's familiar with, he's likelier to notice differences in the rhythm, or the chords, or the voices. He's likelier to appreciate the work of the arranger.'

And when it came to space-age pop, arranging was the name of the game. There seemed to be a competition among the artists to see who could conduct the most outrageous gene-splicing on an old pleasantry like 'Sentimental Journey' or 'Mood Indigo'. Occasionally, efforts sounded contrived; some titles were overdone. After years of studying the genre, these ears ask to be spared further variations on 'Flight of the Bumble Bee', 'Humoresque' or 'Greensleeves'. On the other hand, there's rarely a 'Third Man Theme', 'Hell's Bells' or 'Powerhouse' that fails to satisfy. And it seems almost impossible to make a bad recording of 'Caravan'.

A sense of humour was an essential component of any arranger's skills. Esquivel specialized in sophisticated nose-tweaking, as did the Three Suns. Henry Mancini's Latin send-up of 'Springtime For Hitler' (from the Mel Brooks farce *The Producers*) takes a devastatingly dark joke one step beyond absurdity.

Popular as this music was in the fifties and sixties, it was reviled at the time by hipsters. Why? Here's a good place to start: it was meticulous; the artists and producers were perfectionists. This aesthetic flies in the face of rock'n'roll, which values energy and spontaneity over technique. Yet many examples of space-age pop *rock* – and if they don't rock, they *swing*. (Some do both: 'Julie Is Her Name', by Mambo King Perez Prado was a hybrid style he termed *Rockambo*.) These recordings were made by band leaders and musicians who were young and vibrant, and many of whom were considered upstarts and pioneers. However, space-age pop stopped short of stripped inhibitions; it wasn't intended to induce breathless perspiration. However raucous the arrangements might get, there was always an undercurrent that whispered: 'Relax.'

There were other reasons why this music was dismissed by many of its contemporaries. It was considered Squaresville. *Jeez – trombones and xylophones*! Space-age pop's pedigree can be traced to the elegant big-band ballrooms of the thirties and forties, rather than to the sweaty, decadent R&B joints. It was genetically 'respectable'.

Does that mean this music had no 'soul'? Who cares? Only a pedant with no sense of humour would attempt to address such a question. This music was meant to be festive, to provide a soundtrack for high living.

You don't need a penthouse or a velvet smoking-jacket, a swinging bachelor pad or a track-lit bar in your living-room.

Space-age pop pioneers were a curious and wacky breed. When the spectrum of recorded sound expanded with the advent of high fidelity and stereo, producers, arrangers and band leaders fell over each other plundering the percussion closet. Anything that could be struck with a stick, mallet, pedal, palms, or fingers was in harm's way.

They safaried round the planet trying to outdo each other in discovering exotic rhythm makers: to islands in the South Pacific; from the mountains of Latin America to the Far East; among remote African tribes, through US hobo jungles, and – no doubt – into their own kids' playrooms. If it rattled or went thud, they dragged it into the studio.

They used common, everyday trap sets, tom-toms, bongos and cymbals; kettle drums, congas and tambourines; xylophones and vibraphones. They also called in these instruments' distant cousins and overseas kin – strangers with evocative names like loo jon drum, Chinese bell tree, Tahitian log, marimbula, chromatic bamboo or Burmese gong. Some items mystified: what the heck are 'puppet shakers'? Others led to speculation: could an Indian ankle bells specialist find steady work in Hollywood?

Through clever arrangement and strategic microphone placement, on the beat or off, this hardware would ping-pong, ricochet, spiral, ratchet, whizz by, and occasionally detonate. The policy was: *swing first and ask questions later*.

For the recording sessions of *Orienta*, by the Markko Polo Adventurers, the album liner noted that 'the studio was virtually filled with percussion instruments, as many as twenty-five at one time', played by five players, often doubling up on particular tracks. The overload prompted one drummer to quip, 'Why don't they hire that Oriental god with six or eight arms?'

Original space-age pop records were intended to: 1. satisfy the prodigious sonic appetites of an emerging generation of audiophiles; 2. de-ice their dates; and 3. impress seismologists. Consequently, classic space-age pop albums often went to great lengths to explain technical recording minutiae. Waveform graphs were juxtaposed alongside mic positioning charts, annotated with baffling references to the RIAA crossover curve, feedback cutters, and 500 cps rolloffs. It was the record company's way of assuring the buyer: *We know a lot of things you don't. Trust us – buy this record; it's a technical marvel*. In some cases, arcane jargon lent an LP credibility otherwise lacking in the music. But for the most part, it was obligatory hype, conferring status, and certain to be ignored. Occasionally the fine print could be refreshingly candid. An early Bernie Green album (*More Than You Can Stand In Hi-Fi*, Jazz Records, 1957), after a paragraph of blather about Neumann-Telefunken KM-56 microphones and Pultec Equalizers, noted '. . . In other words, when you put the needle down on the record, it should play, get it? Use the RIAA curve, whatever that means.'

First there was stereo, and then there was stereo action. The difference? Between Minnie Mouse and Gina Lollobrigida. In a word: Va-Va-Voom!

While NASA engineers raced for outer space, RCA engineers raced for aural space. With the introduction of 1961's 'Stereo Action' LP series, RCA proved victorious in beating other record companies to the age of hyperactive two-channel hijinks. (The Russians never even left the compression gate.) While other labels were playing ping-pong with their percussion, RCA was launching inter-groove ballistic mischief on a grand and unprecedented scale.

They heralded stereo action as offering 'spectacular sonic illusions of motion, directionality and depth'. Not content to programme simply for ears, RCA provided a 'visual' component to audio: 'Soloists and entire sections of the orchestra appear to move thrillingly back and forth across the room,' they proclaimed. 'Stereo action is musical movement so real, your eyes will follow the sound.'

When stereo was commerically unveiled in the late fifties, record companies and audio dealers staged a relentless campaign to persuade consumers that two speakers were better than one. Gimmicky demonstration discs were distributed free with the purchase of any home stereo. These LPs featured rifle zings and ping-pong volleys, fireworks, zooming locomotives, and footsteps panning from left channel to right, magically before the astonished listener.

It caught on – for good. Generations later, two channels remain the standard. (In the seventies, they tried four – quadrophonic – but the free market settled the matter: two channels were sufficient. The anatomical configuration of the human head also may have played a small role.) With the stereo action series, RCA made the most of those two channels. Bongos bounced about the den, violins cascaded from the heavens, pianos glided from wall to wall, and vibes chimed as if struck by Tinkerbell's wand.

Too cute? Sensory overload? Stereophonic showing-off? OK, sometimes the producers went overboard with gratuitous cross-channel panning, like kids on Christmas morning playing with a new chemistry set. And – think about it – the image of 'soloists and entire sections of the orchestra appear[ing] to move thrillingly back and forth across the room' is a trifle absurd. The musicians didn't move across the room – thrillingly or otherwise – during their performance; that such an illusion would enhance one's appreciation of an LP was a fanciful marketing ploy. Nevertheless, musical artistry was never a secondary consideration; it was equal with the recording process.

David Hall, music editor of *HiFi/Stereo Review*, in the liner notes to Ray Martin's stereo action entry, *Dynamica*, addressed the question of gimmickry. Referring specifically to the preponderance of ping-pong and choo-choo train demo discs, he observed, 'Wonderful as these stereo sound effects may be as aural novelties, they cannot hold the listener's attention for long or over many hearings. The substance of almost all recordings worth living with is, after all – MUSIC.' And stereo action, he stressed, showcased 'new concepts in the art of orchestral arranging and a large measure of truly imaginative and creative collaboration between musicians and recording engineers'. In other words, it was more than just a fancy canvas – the musical art justified the frame.

For anyone who grew up after 1960, it's difficult to appreciate that advent of wild, apparently three-dimensional sound, especially compared to the monophonic (one-channel) hi-fidelity that came before. Stereo must have seemed a remarkable and mystifying technological achievement – a leap comparable to the advancement from airplanes to moon rockets.

Studio master recordings in those days were captured on three discreet tape channels ('triple-tracking'). To minimize leakage (the sound of one instrument 'bleeding' on to another track), microphones were positioned near instruments with meticulous precision, and the recording signal would be assigned to a particular track. After the performance, the three-track master was mixed down to the left and right channels for home phonographs and tape decks. It was in this post-recording stage that the paning was applied (voila! – *stereo action*). In addition, imbalances and glitches in the master could be corrected by such advances as equalization (filtering out or heightening specific ranges of the sound spectrum), reverberation (a slight echo, for a fuller sound), and adjustment of pitch (via tape speed manipulation), increasing the likelihood that artists and producers wouldn't have to settle for flawed fidelity. The final product was as much a creative expression of the engineer as of the orchestra.

'Every note of the music to be recorded must be scored with stereo action in mind,' the liner notes explained. 'An elaborate system of charting each and every instrument for proper stereo placement guides the actual scoring. In addition to the musical annotation, a companion series of non-musical diagrams for the studio work is developed.'

In addition to the now-you-see-it, now-you-don't arrangements and frolicking percussion, some stereo action albums presented ambitious concepts. Bernie Green's *Furtura*, recorded in 1961, posed the question: 'What will popular music sound like in 1970?' Green's quirky re-tooling of such chestnuts as 'Under Paris Skies' (featuring an electronic device called a 'Tonalyzer') provided some musical clairvoyance.

For Esquivel's *Latin-Esque*, to attain the purest separation of channels, the huge orchestra was divided in half and placed in two studios almost a city block apart, led by two conductors (Esquivel and Stanley Wilson). 'Through an intricate system of inter-communication by headphones,' the

liner notes explained, 'the musicians were able to hear each other and play together just as if they were all in the same room.'

And although Leo Addeo's *The Music Goes 'Round & 'Round* might not be termed a 'concept album', it could be the only orchestral LP to showcase an ocarina trio on every track. (It did not, alas, start a trend though it could have inspired the Troggs's 'Wild Thing').

In an ironic postscript, RCA reissued some stereo action titles in *mono*, a gesture that artist and vinyl enthusiast Wayno compares to 'decolourizing a current hit film for the black and white market'. The record jackets boasted, 'Now for the first time! RCA's acclaimed "Action" series in monoaural hi-fi!'

(Compiled from the sleeve notes from *Space-Age Pop Volumes 1–3*, 1996.)

Max Steiner scored heavy in the movies: *The Informer, Now, Voyager, Since You Went Away, Mildred Pierce, Key Largo, Dark Victory, Gone With The Wind, The Searchers* etc

Max Steiner

A musical prodigy, Steiner graduated from Vienna's Imperial Academy of Music at thirteen, after completing the eight-year course in twelve months. He studied under Mahler before moving to America to work for Florenz Ziegfeld. He began working for the movies with the advent of sound: he won three Oscars (*The Informer*, 1935; *Now, Voyager*, 1942; *Since You Went Away*, 1944), was nominated for a further fifteen, and altogether scored over 200 films (including *Mildred Pierce*, *Key Largo* and *Dark Victory*). His score for *Gone with the Wind* is one of the richest and longest in screen history – there are ninety-nine separate pieces, based on eleven primary motifs, and sixteen additional melodies – whilst his music for *The Searchers* includes a theme for each character.

classic

Swingle Singers

'Largo' (2.58)
Album: Going Baroque (Philips) 1965
Bach has always been easily adapted by the MOR fraternity, and the Swingle Singers almost made a career out of it. Their first album, *Bach's Greatest Hits,* established Ward Swingle's singers as the most adventurous vocal group of their day. This recording (from the Harpsichord Concerto In F Minor) on their follow-up LP is their best work. In 1966 they recorded a breakthrough LP with the Modern Jazz Quartet, *Place Vendôme*, a collaboration which would later inspire Paul Weller during his final days with the Style Council.

Swing Out Sister

For certain types of people, there is no greater epiphany than driving along California's Pacific Coast Highway as Neil Richardson's 'Riviera Affair', Walter Wanderley's 'Rain Forest' or Alan Hawkshaw's 'Girl In A Sportscar' erupts from the car stereo.

It certainly works for Swing Out Sister's Corinne Drewery and Andy Connell. During their twelve-year existence they have dedicated themselves to fusing electro-pop, jazz and funk with their first true love, easy listening. They have moved from clinical pop funk to free-form soul and back again

You've been Swingled. Could voices this sweet have really come from silly old Earth?

while always retaining a keen pop sensibility. Their first LP, 1987's *It's Better To Travel*, contained a clutch-bag of hit singles – 'Blue Mood', 'Breakout', 'Surrender' – though it was 1989's euphoric *Kaleidoscope World* which firmly established their lounge credentials. Containing beautiful songs such as 'You On My Mind', 'Forever Blue', 'Where In The World' and 'Coney Island Man', the album was a love letter to luxury, a paean to the five-star pop days of yore. In fact 'Coney Island Man' was almost an homage to Bacharach himself, and worthy of inclusion in any great sixties espionage movie involving a coastline drive (the Riviera, the Santa Monica Freeway, Sorrento, wherever), an implausibly sunny day and a flame-coloured open-top sportscar driven by a wispy blonde in a Jackie O headscarf and Argentine air-hostess sunglasses.

'Personally,' says Andy Connell, 'I have a real problem relating to things like James Brown or Motown because it's nothing to do with me. I never listened to that when I was growing up. I bought records by Burt Bacharach.' 'Forever Blue' even uses a refrain borrowed from John Barry's theme for *Midnight Cowboy*. 'We called him up and told him what we were up to and he said he didn't mind,' says Corinne. On this track, and another from the same LP, 'Precious Words', SOS drew on the talents of Jimmy Webb, and Connell was in shock for weeks afterwards: 'He was astonishing; he took these songs and transformed them . . . when he was in the studio I was literally speechless.'

'I find it difficult to form opinions about a lot of modern music because my head's buried in the past,' says Corinne. 'A lot of my favourite records seem to have been picked up in the discount rack in Woolworth's. I'll be quite happy if our records end up in the Woollies bargain bin in ten years' time.'

Swing Out Sister manage to delve into the past without becoming corny or overtly mannered. For them, the records are not totems of some trash aesthetic; theirs is not an ironic stance – they never wanted to be ABC or the Mike Flowers Pops – yet they still seem distanced from the pop music they make so well. They say they can't put their finger on why. Encapsulating youth has never been their aim – they'll never write 'All The Young Dudes' or 'Saturday Night Beneath The Plastic Palm Trees' – but in an age of endlessly recycled rebellion this is probably just as well. They have diversified these past few years, and with albums such as *Get In Touch With Yourself* and *The Living Return* have explored the rather more fluid attributes of soul and jazz. They remain, however, something of an enigma, and certainly light years away from the copycat groups trying to jump on the easy bandwagon. The missing link between Francis Lai and Curtis Mayfield, between Martin Denny and Tania Maria, the Ohio Players and Burt Bacharach, for the time being the bargain bins will be fine without them. Swing *out* supperclub!

Can you hear me, darling, Can you hear the SOS? Swing Out Sister's classic tracks include 'Blue Mood', 'You On My Mind', 'Forever Blue', 'Twilight World', 'Where In The World', 'Coney Island Man', 'Get In Touch With Yourself', 'Am I The Same Girl?', 'Precious Words', 'Feel Free' etc

classic

Swing Out Sister
'Coney Island Man' (3.44)
Album: The Kaleidoscope World (Phonogram) 1989
A modern companion piece to Bacharach's 'Pacific Coast Highway' by pop's easycore mavericks.

classic

Swing Out Sister
'You On My Mind' (3.32)
Single (Mercury) 1991
Sixties' easy-listening pop given a sophisticated eighties' refurbishment by a group who fully understand the importance of genuine MOR. A day trip to nirvana (Arcadia can wait until tomorrow).

The Theremin
Look Ma, no hands! The theremin, invented by the Russian Leon Theremin in New York during the Depression, is fundamentally a small wooden box complete with two antennae – one controlling the volume, the other controlling the pitch – around which the player waves his or her hands. One of the earliest electronic instruments, sounds were created by the radio waves excited by the wire antennae. It became a staple of many

Leon Theremin's 'ether wave' device evoked a sound of the ancient Sirens, according to some, and became an all-too regular feature on science fiction soundtracks, most noticeably in *The Day The Earth Stood Still*

a sci-fi soundtrack; used to great effect by Les Baxter, Clara Rockmore, Samuel Hoffman and Robert Moog in the fifties and sixties, and by Captain Beefheart and Tangerine Dream in the seventies, the theremin has recently been embraced by Portishead, Tricky and Jamiroquai.

Robert Moog, who invented the legendary analog Minimoog synthesizer in 1971 – thus changing the face and form of modern electronic music – experimented with theremins from an early age. He built his first model at the age of fourteen, wrote many articles on how to construct them, incorporated those ideas into his own work, and eventually began producing the machines commercially. 'You do need training [to play one],' he says. 'It's an élitist instrument, because if you contrast it to something like a guitar or a ukulele or accordion or piano, there are few people who have the talent to be able to even get a melody out of it. It takes thousands of hours to get really good.'

classic

Jackie Trent
'Where Are You Now' (2.44)
Single (Pye) 1965
Trent's ex-husband Tony Hatch recorded various instrumental interpretations of his song, though this remains the definitive version. Conjuring up images of battered Sunbeam Alpines cruising down country lanes covered in dappled sunlight, this is quite possibly the most evocative record ever made. 'When shadows of evening gently fall, the memory of you I soon recall . . .'

Trip-Hop
Once described as a genre based on taking old John Barry singles and playing them at sixteen rpm, Trip-Hop is the spooky sound of hip-hop falling over classic movie soundtracks. Bristol's Portishead are Britain's biggest exponents, leading a trip-hop charge that includes Tricky, Massive Attack, Beastie Boys collaborator Money Mark and literally scores of people associated with the Mo' Wax label. According to *Q*, 'It's slow – decelerated "Theme From *Mission Impossible*" with girl singing about death over the top, or ruthlessly minimalist breakbeats plus plangent sample deployment for mood of abstraction.'

'It's slow – Decelerated "Theme From Mission Impossible" with girl singing about death over the top, or ruthlessly minimalist breakbeats plus plangent sample deployment for mood of abstraction'

Juxtaposition or embellishment? 'If you want some really eerie sound to go along with something, which is the kind of stuff I'm into,' says Portishead figurehead Geoff Barrow, 'What usually happens is people use pre-sets on a synthesizer. They get the little M-1 and it says "spooky sound", so you go [press] like that, and there's your weird sound. But what they were doing on those old soundtracks was using mechanical instruments like Rhodes pianos, Wurlitzers and Hammonds, and making them come out with weird noises and delays. Recording a bit of tape, looping stuff up, taking it backwards. To me, that's where you develop your *own* sounds. You're not playing some sound made up by the Korg Corporation.'

Scott Walker

It used to be that there was nothing more fashionable than outsiders, those misfits on the margins who avoided convention like the plague. Their trajectory was simple: starburst entry, rapid disillusionment, then a life spent in the shadows producing work which in years to come is seen as their most challenging and enlightening. Cult heroes, they were called, and though most of them have by now been exposed to daylight (a process starting with lavish journalistic praise and ending in histrionic biopics), some are still with us, lurking in dark corners of their own making.

Scott Walker has spent the best part of the last twenty-five years on the margins, certainly on the edges of the pop world and seemingly on the verges of the real one, too. He has honed tortured, existential angst to such a degree that his haunting, desperate records can alter the mood of a room as surely as a power cut. His is a twilight world, but hardly a pretentious one; dozens of devotees have tried to emulate Walker's style and attitude over the years, yet Walker remains a true original. Whereas you get the feeling that the people who try and copy him are just affecting a pose, with Walker it's difficult to imagine him doing anything else. 'I do believe I'm an artist,' says Walker, 'and what I do is important. But not everyone has to hear it, and I don't need to do it all the time.'

It is the summer of 1995, and Walker is talking in the quiet confines of his manager's four-storey terraced house in the heart of London's Holland Park. Here, amongst the organized clutter of children's toys, pop videos and overburdened bookshelves, he is explaining just what he has been up to since 1984, when he released *Climate Of Hunter*. This is only his second interview in eleven years – organized to promote the *Tilt* LP – yet he is unusually forthcoming and answers accusations of drunkenness, tardiness and downright perversion with grace. His cheeks are a little flushed, but he looks remarkable for a fifty-one-year-old who admits to a rather combustible relationship with drink and drugs.

'I still drink, but nowhere near as much as I did,' Walker says. 'There was drink and all kinds of other stuff. I used to really go for it, drinking more and more just because I hated what I was doing. It started towards the end of the [Walker] Brothers but continued right into my solo career as I battled against people trying to push my career in directions I didn't want it to go. They wanted me to be Perry Como and I wouldn't do it. They wanted me to be Mick Jagger – I wouldn't do it.'

In the mid-sixties the Walker Brothers were about as big as a pop group could be. Ohio-born Scott Engel teamed up with Gary Leeds and John Maus to form the Walker Brothers in 1964, but it was only when they left California for England twelve months later that they had any kind of success.

During the next two years they became as famous as the Rolling Stones, the Kinks or the Who, recording a series of spectacularly successful melodramatic torch songs which owed much to Phil Spector – 'The Sun Ain't Gonna Shine Anymore', 'My Ship Is Coming In', 'Make It Easy On Yourself' – all sung in Scott Walker's soaring baritone. Their material was a manageable mix of the light and the dark, but when Walker went solo in 1967, the dark side came to the fore. His first solo singles were hits, though the success tailed off as he found it increasingly difficult to balance the Radio 2 ballads which he performed on the TV show he fronted, with the maudlin and esoteric workings of his LPs (he became obsessed with Jacques Brel, recording dozens of his songs). Devastated by the commercial failure of his 1969 LP *Scott 4*, he all but walked off into the sunset. In the process he became the cult hero to end them all.

Walker went solo not only because of the increasing squabbles within the group, but also because he was ill-equipped to deal with the demands of pop celebrity; he had a pathological fear of performing live, and recoiled from the 'screamagers' – as he called them – who fell adoringly at his feet.

Towards the end of 1966, at the height of the group's fame, Walker moved to a Benedictine monastery on the Isle of Wight, but within days the island was awash with teenage girls, demanding their idol. 'I loathe

the show business ladder and the way it operates,' he said at the time. 'I only do it for the bread.'

'I was always more interested in following a pure path than most people,' says Walker, carefully, as if he's unsure about what I'm going to do with this information. 'To me, singing like Sinatra or Tony Bennett was more of a divine path than anything the hippies got up to in the sixties. All those longhairs were morally bankrupt, they were acting as though the real world didn't actually exist. I wanted to be a totally serious torch singer, someone who is dedicated to their craft; I didn't want to stand in front of thousands of young girls, whipping them into a frenzy, nor did I want to pretend I came from Mars. All I wanted to do was sing my songs.'

Along with David Hemmings, Simon Dee and David Bailey he once seemed the epitome of mid-sixties chic, but Walker soon retreated into himself, shunning his fans, his fame, and eventually himself. There were reports of heroin addiction and attempted suicides . . . but above all else was the music. The Walker Brothers reformed in the middle of the seventies, having some success with the song 'No Regrets', but after another few years of intermittent recording, Scott drifted off again.

'I've been painting and drawing a lot [for three years in the late eighties he attended the Byam Shaw School of Art in South London], and keeping myself to myself. I was always torn between being a painter and a musician, so I picked it up when I was at a loose end. I've also travelled a bit, but basically I've had a very low profile.

'I signed this new deal two years ago, and it was great because Mercury Records gave me *carte blanche* to go and do exactly what I wanted to. I think people have now realized that it's no good trying to get me to do something else because it always ends in frustration for both parties. I know I'm difficult, but I also know what makes me happy. In the years between my last record and this one there have been lots of solitary times, times without much money and even less motivation, but at least I haven't been pressurized to do things I didn't want to.'

By the time of *Climate Of The Hunter* Walker was looked after by Dire Straits's manager Ed Bicknell who, after the record's release, tried to get his charge to record an album of songs written by the likes of Chris Difford and Glen Tilbrook from Squeeze, Mark Knopfler and Boy George. Predictably this came to nothing, as did a collaboration with Brian Eno and Daniel Lanois.

'A lot of people have tried to reactivate my career, but I always found them too contrived,' says Walker, with no reluctance at all. 'I've got no interest in nostalgia. There was a misunderstanding between Eno, Lanois and myself on that particular record. I spent six months writing material and then brought it into the studio to record with them, but I found their way of working too scattered, and Lanois I found totally useless. So one

night in the very early stages of making the record I just stood up and walked out.'

It's fashionable at the moment to say that There Is No Weird Anymore, but you've only got to listen to *Tilt* to know that this patently isn't true. Modern industrial mood music for cold winter evenings in dark Eastern European cities, *Tilt* makes Leonard Cohen seem like the Chipmunks. Self-possessed and grim, it's a difficult and mannered record, but ultimately a rewarding one, and perhaps the only one Walker could make.

'With *Tilt* I've tried to achieve neutrality. I've been trying for sounds that have never been heard before. I rarely hear songs and wish I'd written them, you know. I know that sounds arrogant, but I find most pop songs difficult to listen to because I find melody such an overrated thing. Whenever I write a song these days, and I find myself getting too melodious, I stop and pull back a bit.'

Was the thought of re-entering the media circus after all these years a bit daunting?

'The thought of becoming public property again definitely stopped me from finishing the record. The pressure is still there, like, when are you going to do a concert, when are you going to do television? Unfortunately, being the kind of person I am I can only take one thing at a time.'

And how does he feel about being regarded as the cult hero to end them all?

'I don't feel negative about it, but I don't *know* a lot of it. I'm flattered by the attention, and I'd rather have it than not have it, though it somehow feels as though it's happening to someone else . . .'

So just how much pathos is there here? If Walker doesn't seem too perturbed about his situation, then who does?

'Believe me,' says Walker, on the edge of his seat at last, 'I'm not bitter, I've rarely been resentful and I'm really very happy with my lot in life. But it hasn't always been easy . . . I just believe there are certain standards in life, and I like to try and keep to them. In terms of my ambitions I'm not sure that I have any left.

'Have you got enough?'

Scott Walker
'Windows Of The World' (4.21)
Album: Scott 2 (Philips) 1968
Black with gold trim. A fairly straightforward cover of the Bacharach & David song by the music business's most reluctant torch singer. Perhaps what the world needs now is not love, sweet love, but another Scott Walker record.

Dionne Warwick

by John Bowers

She sat in the Scepter Records studio in the Times Square area like girls do in church pews with head up, hands folded on lap, a shy look on her face. She wore mod white stockings, a tight brown skirt and a sweater two sizes too small. To the white visitor she spoke about a group called the Drinkard Singers. 'My mother sang with them, and I used to trail along to the churches and schools where they performed. My uncles and aunts were in the group, too.' She pronounced 'aunts' as in 'haunts'.

She told about her travels to Europe, and commented on other black entertainers. 'I really admire Josephine Baker. The way she took in all these little kids from different nationalities and has them living together on this big estate. They're growing up without any hate or bickering or anything like that. When I saw them all living together like that, it was the most beautiful thing I had ever seen.'

When tired-looking musicians began arriving, Dionne Warwick rose to start rehearsing a new nightclub act. Passing through a control room, filled with coloured lights, microphones and multiple knobs, Dionne ran across Chuck Jackson, a handsome, oak-skinned singer in a green cardigan. 'Umm, baby,' he said, eyes roving, 'you sure change since you been to Europe.'

'Yeah? Like I gain weight?'

'That's all right. What I see, that's all right.'

'You talk.'

'Yeah, you sure fulfil yourself in Europe, baby. Just like you fill

'The play of this voice makes you think of an eel, of a storm, of a cradle, a knot of seaweed, a dagger,' wrote one French critic of Dionne Warwick. 'It is not so much a voice as an organ. You could write figures for Warwick's voice'

that skirt.' They laughed, slapping their legs, making a sound like 'whoowee!' Paul Cantor, Dionne's manager, moved around with a cardboard container of coffee. He chuckled a little, but did not slap his leg nor make a 'whoowee!' sound. Burt Bacharach, who has composed the music for all of Dionne's hits ('Don't Make Me Over', 'Anyone Who Had a Heart', 'Walk On By', 'Message to Michael') was not there that evening. He was married to Angie Dickinson, a blonde, peaches-and-cream actress, and they were then in London. Dionne did not see him so much now that he was married.

Bacharach had first met Dionne when she was doing background singing for the Drifters and going to Hartt College in Connecticut. He composed Dionne's first solo, 'Don't Make Me Over', a weepy number addressed to an offstage lover:

> Don't make me over now that
> I'd do anything for you
> Don't make me over now that
> You know how I adore you
> Just take me for what I am
> Accept me for what I am.

Bacharach – young, volatile, engaging – has always been closely identified with her musical style and life. 'I get along well with his parents,' Dionne says. 'Even now, after his marriage. They treat me like one of the family . . .'

Dionne once played the organ in church and sang in the choir. She has combed the South, a member of an unusual troupe. She would be hired in Atlanta along with thirty other entertainers for thirty-one days, and then booked into as many towns as humanly possible. They travelled solely by bus, often going two days without sleeping in a bed. She has driven to Nova Scotia from New Jersey to play a one-night stand. She has jetted to Bermuda, Puerto Rico and across the Atlantic many times to sing her songs and pick up her paychecks. A few months ago she appeared on *Hullabaloo*, a feat she takes quite casually now.

The show was video-taped in a barnlike structure in the depths of Brooklyn. Teeny boppers crowded the entrance, screeching and clutching autograph pads. Inside, Dionne went through her number with a scarf over her head, her dress hitting just above her knees.

One stagehand spotted Dionne frugging in the elevated cage that *Hullabaloo* uses to house female dancers. 'Boy, look at that big coloured gal go! Am I getting an eyeful!'

Dionne, in turn, spotted the stagehand, and went to a dressing-room to put a pair of slacks under her dress. She signed autographs for three little white girls coming back, and a grey-haired black janitor looked at the tableau in puzzlement and pride. During a break in rehearsals, Dionne nibbled on a limp chicken salad sandwich to the side of the set. The night before she had gone to bed at five at home in East Orange, New Jersey, and had arisen at seven for the *Hullabaloo* show. Slight circles under her eyes, forcing another bite of food down, she reminisced about Sacha Distel.

She had met him while both performed for a TV show in London. He had black hair, pale skin, a crinkly smile and was taller than he looked. He came right up and said, 'I'm Sacha Distel. I'd like to get to know you.' In a sort of trance she found herself still with him that evening, indeed getting to know him.

She was staying at the Mayfair, but the management wouldn't let Sacha upstairs. The two of them then spent the entire night in the downstairs lounge, talking. She found herself suddenly babbling things she had never dared utter before, and he told her a lot about himself. He was like no other person she had ever met before – black or white. Shortly after dawn he left to fly to another city. But before he boarded the plane, he sent her two dozen roses.

'With Sacha everything is wham wham,' Lee Valentine, a background guitarist for Dionne, said later. 'He's one of the few white men I've ever met who made me forget the race thing. A white from New York would be too polite, too liberal, never tell me what's really on his mind. A white Southern guy might try to knock my teeth out. But Sacha – he wasn't phony. He saw something he wanted, he went after it . . .'

But problems, problems – even in France. Soon after meeting Sacha, Dionne was appearing with him at the Olympia in Paris and one day called his home. A woman answered. 'Let me speak to Sacha,' Dionne said.

'Who's this?'

'Who you? You his mother?'

'I'm his wife.'

When Dionne collared him, he said, 'It's not important. I would have told you if I'd thought it was important . . .'

Dionne encountered other women who knew Sacha. Once backstage at the Olympia a chauffeur in livery entered her dressing-room to say that Brigitte Bardot would like to see her. Blonde, blue-eyed, she came in. Dionne likes to remember now that she really didn't know who she was. 'Tony Perkins had been backstage, and I knew who he was. Lots of big stars had dropped by. B.B. didn't mean a thing to me then.'

They chatted. Recalling the dialogue now, Dionne gets the better of it. 'I hear you go with a Frenchman,' Bardot said.

'I know a lot of Frenchmen.'

'I mean *my* Frenchman.'

'You mean Sacha? I guess you right, baby. Only he my Frenchman now.'

It solves problems to believe you bested the Sex Kitten, that you know more how to handle a charmer than the Sex Goddess of the Western World. 'Sacha could have married B.B. anytime he wanted and she would have supported him. She was crazy for him. But he wanted to do his own *supporting*. She went around with him when all he had was a guitar and no money. She couldn't wait, and by the time he was a success it was too late. She never understood him.'

Later, Dionne would proudly play an album she and Sacha recorded at the Olympia. She would display a photo of him which he had signed affectionately. She would happily tell of plans they had to tour together.

But an actress, who had made movies in Europe, said, 'Oh, God, don't tell me about *another one* Sacha's captivated. Europe's filled with them …'

On a crisp spring night she drove her black Cadillac convertible down the Jersey turnpike for home. In fifteen minutes her taped performance on *Hullabaloo* was to be shown on TV, and she kept a heavy foot on the accelerator. Willie, her personal valet, rode with her and dourly predicted that they would be late.

'*I* miss one of my TV shows? *I* be right on time!'

A slender, ramrod-straight youth, Willie had met Dionne when she was singing with the Atlanta-based concert touring company and he was selling programmes. At that time Dionne was travelling with her mother, and Willie began carrying their luggage because he had always got along well with 'older women'. When Dionne became affluent, she moved Willie to East Orange, New Jersey, to be her constant companion and full-time valet. He picks up wigs she has ordered, lays out dresses and gowns for her performances, and stands guard in her backstage dressing-room. He is also allowed in the room while she is dressing.

Dionne eased the Cadillac beside a corner two-storey house on a quiet middle-class street. She greeted family, friends who had dropped by, and got before the colour TV in the den just as *Hullabaloo* flashed on the screen. Her image in a head scarf came on and sang 'Message to Michael'. After a short pause, family and friends complimented her. 'Wow, you way out of sight on this one!'

Then everyone moved through the house toward a huge meal. In the living-room a greenish artificial tree pretended to grow, high-school graduation pictures of dark faces in white robes rested on the mantel, and everything was neatly placed and in order. In the well-lit dining-room clear protective plastic covered the chair bottoms, and heaping plates of chicken, spare ribs, cabbage, potatoes, greens and hot rolls rose from the table. Everyone got a big cola to drink with a glass of ice by his plate, but no alcohol. A white visitor, a guest in the house for the first time, bit into a chicken leg as every other head suddenly dropped and Dionne said grace, ending reverently with, 'for Christ's sake'.

Dionne's mother, a light-skinned, youthful woman, circled the table serving food. A younger brother Mancel (Pookie) kept his head ducked over his food, seemingly shy before strangers. Although reputed to have a fine singing voice, nothing has ever prevailed upon him to let loose in public. Dionne's father, a cook at the Masters School in Dobbs Ferry, comes home on weekends and was not here that evening. Dionne's sister DeeDee – plumper, darker than Dionne and herself a professional singer – talked of European travel and the way to wangle good bookings. Names such as James Brown, Chubby Checker, the Shirelles, the Supremes filled the air. Safe motels and restaurants in show-business towns were discussed, and personal experience related. Dionne hugged her tiny dog, Bang Bang, against her chest and let its small pink tongue dart against her cheek. A feeling emanated from the dining table that women made the rules in this house and brought in the big paychecks.

During coffee Dionne played the album of her and Sacha. 'You sure he's tall enough?' said DeeDee good-naturedly.

'Sure he is. You think I don't know how tall he is.'

Dionne's mother, who listened stoically to the recording, was asked what she thought of Sacha. 'Sacha? I don't know that to think of Sacha.'

At midnight Dionne drove a few blocks to her apartment, a safe, brick and glass structure. She emerged in black fur, black slacks and high black boots and drove to the Playbill Club downtown in East Orange, listening to early-hour radio music and speaking of Timmy Brown, the Philadelphia Eagle back. 'When I'm playing a gig down in Philly, we're together. And he comes up to New York now and then. He has tantrums every once in a while, and they say I'm the only girl knows how to handle him. We understand each other. But, you know, like we've never been more than good friends.'

The Playbill Club had white management, black customers and could have been snatched five minutes before from Harlem. Men wore their hats at the circular bar and women in finery sat primly on the stools. On a platform in the middle of the bar a group played jazz, sweat popping from the one on solo. Only the neat drummer with straight black hair and grayish brown skin played impassively, not glancing Dionne's way. She ordered a double Jack Daniels with ginger ale and lemon.

As the male group knocked themselves out, people flocked to Dionne, arms around her, kissing her on the cheek, proud in the way that only minorities can be proud of someone who has made it. 'You do it big in Europe, baby?'

'I get by. Hey, set these folks up with drinks, bartender!'

Near closing time the handsome drummer played his solo. Still keeping an impassive façade and looking straight ahead, he flailed away as if driving an animus from his soul.Then, for the first time that evening, he turned and looked Dionne full in the face. His name was Bill Elliott and he passed sometimes as her husband – 'Look, there's *Dionne Warwick*'s husband going there!' Teenage magazines printed that they were married, fans glimpsed him going in and out of her apartment on occasion, and even Paul Cantor, Dionne's manager, didn't know if they were wed or not. Their relationship dated back to the time when Dionne was only a leggy girl in high-school and Bill was the sporty drummer in the clubs. Then it had been – 'Look, there's *Bill*'s girl going there!'

Now as the lights turned up, the white management counted money, and Willie's sleepy head lolled. Dionne and Bill secluded themselves in a back room. Later, Bill walked her to her long black Cadillac convertible. 'You want to go up to Boston with me sometime this week?' he said.

'I don't think so. Got a lot to do.'

'I'll call you to see if you change your mind.'

'Not going to be home much this week.'

'I'll keep trying.'

'Listen, I give you a ring, Okay?'

'When I marry you,' he said, laughing to take the edge off, 'you'll do like I say.'

It was three o'clock in the morning, and he walked off down a dark street while Dionne screeched into a U-turn and shot toward the George Washington Bridge. She was going to stay at the Americana Hotel that night in order to be near an early morning appointment. She could afford it. 'He likes to gamble too much,' she said, gesturing toward East Orange, 'and I'm not sure we can make it work. The man I marry has to support me!'

Dionne went back on the road. She appeared before many dissimilar audiences. In Washington she sang in the dignified décor of Howard University's Crampton Auditorium. Decked out in a hip-hugging turquoise gown, she bantered with the black audience, sang her usual songs, played 'This Little Light Of Mine' on the piano. They whistled and roared at her wiggly walk, cheered her singing. An entourage filled her dressing-room while fans waited outside for her autograph. In a downstairs reception area she tried to wolf down *hors d'oeuvres*, but a phalanx of university students with programmes and pencils drove her to the wall.

At midnight she ate a steak (very well done) in a depersonalized dining-room of the Washington Hilton. With a combo playing show tunes, waiters making flourishes over water glasses and hosts beaming at neatly dressed black patrons, high prices could be expected to follow as the night the day. Dionne contemplated the Jack Daniels she had felt duty bound to order. 'You know, I really hate this drink. I just started drinking it because Burt Bacharach said what terrific stuff it was.'

An incongruous German waiter in a starched red jacket lit her cigarette and gently enquired into her preference for salad sauce. Dionne told him, somewhat uncomfortable with his blond head hovering over her. When she went up to her room she found that she had been locked out. Through a clerical mistake the room had been rented to someone else while she was performing at Howard University and no other room was available. The management was terribly sorry, apologizing every other sentence and secured a motel room for her in Virginia. Before leaving at three-thirty a.m. for the drive to Arlington, she autographed a message for a black security guard. The black porter's eyes rose and fell like the coloured bouncing ball in bars as she walked to the car that would take her to Virginia and a single bed.

Early next morning she flew to New York with a copy of *Mademoiselle* on her lap. 'I read comic books when I'm alone. *Patsy* and *Milly the Model* . . .'

Peter Matz, the musical arranger, was to see her at ten o'clock, and she feared being late. 'He does arrangements for Barbra Streisand. Did you see her TV special? Boy, if I can get him to work for me!'

Running late at Newark airport, she rented a Hertz at a stand where all the girls knew her. They complimented her on her *Hullabaloo* performance.

'And your husband came through the airport the other day. My, he's something!'

'Yeah, he is.'

Dionne had to wait a couple of bleak hours in a scarred rehearsal room on Eighth Avenue for the man who had arranged Barbra Streisand's TV special, and at the interim ate half a delicatessen sandwich. At her Basin Street East opening in April, Peter Matz was given credit outside for the arrangements.

The audience that night had its fill of luminaries. Ella Fitzgerald and Miles Davis among others were introduced. Choked up at the sight of so many celebrities, Dionne's light man and road manager introduced her as Dionne 'Warren' – and was subsequently sacked. She came out in a simple pinkish gown, nervous herself, and let fly. When she sang standards that Barbra Streisand could have done, the audience shifted uncomfortably. Finally, though, when she hit on the gospel bluesy numbers, a change went through the crowd that even the waiters hustling drinks respected.

Spread your wings for New Orleans –
Kentucky Bluebird,
Fly away – and take a message
to Michael, message to Michael.
He sings each night in some café –
in his search to find wealth and fame
I hear Michael has gone and
changed his name –

Her family and Bill Elliott sat at a prominent table, and they followed behind Ella Fitzgerald and Miles Davis to her dressing-room in opening-night euphoria. Months later Dionne said, 'Miles came around to the dressing room every night I was at Basin Street and brought champagne. I still don't know why he did it except that's the way he is. He used to upset all the people back there using those "f" words all the time. But that's the way Miles is.'

From Basin Street Dionne went to one-night stands on college campuses, to a Catskill resort and in late June appeared at the Steel Pier in Atlantic City. In an environment where the sinking are plucked hourly from the sea and tottering citizens warm wrinkled skin for perhaps the last summer, Dionne sang about love and lovers. Throughout her performance men with canes and women with varicose veins shuffled out. Backstage in her dressing-room Willie kept her company as a handful of teenyboppers passed through for her autograph. There was no need for Dionne to hurry outside, for only sunbathing, saltwater taffy and remote pink faces waited.

'Guess what?' I got married a couple of weeks ago, and I'm not lying this time. We really made it official. Here's the ring to prove it.'

What about Europe? What about Sacha?

She shrugged. 'I'm going to tour Australia.'

Later in the summer she played to a sell-out crowd in Wollman Rink in Central Park. Two thousand fans who couldn't get tickets listened from park benches, grass and rocks around the rink. As helicopters and jets passed overhead, and the moon shone just west of the Pierre Hotel, Dionne sang her numbers and the audience in bell bottomed slacks and Ben Franklin specs was with her.

Policemen guarded her dressing-room area against the sea of long hair and poor-boy sweaters. That night in Central Park was when they loved you. And if they said they loved you (and you could sing or dance or box well enough) they would fly you to Rome, Paris or Sydney. But after your act came the bleak summer afternoons in Atlantic City, the grey mornings alone in London.　　　　　　　　　　　(Published in *The Golden Bowers,* 1971.)

classic

Dionne Warwick
'Valley Of The Dolls' (3.30)
Single (Pye International) 1968
Warwick's filigree voice sounds here like it's about to expire. This record is so sad it can break your heart without even trying, time and time again – surely the most skilfully arranged suicide note ever recorded.

Jimmy Webb

by Giles Smith

Everybody knows a Jimmy Webb tune. Maybe 'By The Time I Get To Pheonix' or 'MacArthur Park'. Maybe 'Galveston', or 'Wichita Lineman'. Definitely 'Up Up And Away' ('in my beautiful balloon . . .'). And all sorts of singers have recorded one – Tony Bennett, Liza Minnelli, Glen Campbell, Donna Summer. In a career not short of astonishing successes and clinching moments, Webb has but one chief regret. That album of his songs by Frank Sinatra – whatever happened to it?

After all, the two of them are more than casually acquainted. Right from early on, whenever Sinatra stood on a stage and sang 'Didn't We', he was sure to announce, 'This is by the young American songwriter, Jimmy Webb'. And Webb has a neat stock of Sinatra stories, like the time he visited Frank in his riverside New York apartment and Sinatra turned from gazing out of the window and said, 'You know, it's a lot further from Hoboken to Manhattan than it looks'. But for twenty years now, they've been talking about that album, and it's never come off. For which we must join Webb in laying a substantial portion of the blame at the door of his dad.

'Sinatra was playing Vegas and I went up to his suite and played some tunes for him. He said, "Let's have dinner later at the Jockey Club. Is anyone here with you?" I said, "Yes, Mr Sinatra. As a matter of fact, my father's here." He said, "Why don't you bring him along?" So we meet at the Jockey Club. Now my father was a marine during World War II, was in the South Pacific, and this is like totally unreal for him that he's sitting at the same table as Frank Sinatra. And I'm counting on talking a lot of business and pursuing this ephemeral album of Jimmy Webb stuff that never seems to happen. Instead, he gets into it with my dad. He must have talked to my father solidly for an hour and a half like old pals, about the war, about Glenn Miller, and I'm left going, What happened to my

133

meeting? 'Those guys,' he says, mournful for a minute. 'They have a way of talking – Hey, schweetheart, how are ya? Hey Jimmy baby, how ya doin? Style is going out, that Humphrey Bogart thing. It's almost like Sinatra is the last of a kind.'

And you could say the same about Jimmy Webb, a writer who came out of soul and rock and pop and who made his money in the sixties, but whose work found acceptance with some of the American Greats: Sammy Kahn, Johnny Mercer, Jules Styne. He's got a foot on both sides of the divide. When Webb goes, a link with the past goes with him.

Now though, at forty-seven, he's busy working from a studio on Broadway in New York, at the more sober, downtown end, rather than along the ritzy midtown section. In a booming, high-ceilinged room where the air-conditioning roars mercilessly, there's a grand piano, some keyboards and a large quantity of recording paraphernalia. At one end sits Mr Webb's assistant, cordoned off behind a pasteboard wall which functions as Webb's memo board and rogues' gallery.

Here are notes reading 'Songs needed: Bonnie Raitt' and, cryptically, 'Tony Bennett: Robin in touch w/d to arrange.' A prominent sticker declares, 'It's Sinatra's world: we just live in it'. Here's a picture of his friend Linda Ronstadt's pet calf, Sweet Pea. Here's Webb's pink 'McGovern '72' campaign T-shirt, worn to a feather and, inexplicably, a signed picture of Mike Baldwin from *Coronation Street*.

Webb sits on a black sofa under this ragged display and, peering through his cigarette smoke, talks earnestly and in a slow drawl about his extraordinary career.

He had started writing songs in the mid-sixties at High School in San Bernadino, California, and, still a student, he would drive into LA to pitch them at publishers. Strangely, he first struck lucky at Jobete, the publishing division of Motown. 'The first friendly face I saw was black. They gave me money for schoolbooks and gasoline.' He got his first track away on a Supremes Christmas album ('That was my first cheque') but it wasn't enough to pay the rent, so he got a job sweeping up at a studio on Melrose Avenue and wrote lead sheets (transcriptions of melodies for musicians who cannot write music) for five dollars a whack.

Then he got a job as a rehearsal pianist and vocal arranger for a singing group called the Versatiles and one day, when the band leader was out of town, he sneaked in one of his own compositions. It began: 'Would you like to ride in my beautiful balloon? Would you like to glide in my beautiful balloon . . .'

'I had written it in a practice room in San Bernadino Valley college and I wasn't supposed to be in there. They didn't allow songwriting in the practice rooms, so I was writing it and looking over my shoulder to see if I

'By the time I was twenty-one, I had accomplished all the goals I had set for myself for a lifetime,' says Jimmy Webb. 'You have all this energy left and you don't know exactly what to do with it. You find yourself saying: "What am I going to do tomorrow?"'

134

was about to get thrown out of the building.' The Versatiles became the 5th Dimension, 'Up Up And Away' came out on the Soul City label, and a year later, Webb was collecting five Grammy Awards, not to mention some startling royalty cheques. It was 1967. He was twenty-one.

'I remember back then that if you didn't make $600 in a year, you didn't have to pay taxes or file a tax return. I went from a year of no filing a tax return to $50,000 the next year.' He moved – as you would – into what had once been the Philippine Embassy in LA and started partying. 'It was a lovely big place in a doomed, authentic Hollywood neighbourhood – a building with a tiled roof, tied floors, chandeliers, carved staircases, bathrooms with these glorious thirties tiles, greens and blacks. I moved in there with about thirty of my friends. We lived commune-style.'

Some rum coves passed through Webb's Embassy during those times. Tiny Tim used to come over all the time; Jimi Hendrix spent the night there at least once. 'People knew you could come there if you needed something to eat or somewhere to crash. One day, there was a guy at the door with two women and a picnic basket asking for something to eat. I went down to the kitchen and someone was making sandwiches for them. I stuck out my hand and said, "Hi, I'm Jimmy." And he says, "Hi, I'm Charlie Manson." Wasn't until years later that it came crashing in on me.'

Webb carried on composing. He wrote 'By The Time I Get To Phoenix', which Glen Campbell recorded and which has since appeared in at least twenty-six other versions, and is the third most performed song in the world after 'Never My Love' and 'Yesterday'. He then wrote 'Wichita Lineman' as a follow-up, inspired by the sight of a man up a telegraph pole in a vast, otherwise unoccupied landscape in Oklahoma. It took him an afternoon.

'Seemed too easy. I didn't expect much to come of it.' Actually, it helped him start a collection of cars: two Stringrays, two Eldorados, a Maserati, a Camaro . . .

Webb didn't meet Campbell until after their third hit together, the anti-war song 'Galveston'. 'We met at someone else's session. He walked in, looked at me and said, "Huh, when you gonna get a haircut?" Politically, we were on opposite sides of the fence – he had that big TV show, really short hair, was carrying the banner of Republican conservatism and having John Wayne on his show. I didn't appreciate that exactly at the time, but we became loyal friends. He's been there for me through the ups and downs and he has always recorded my stuff.'

In late 1968, somewhat the worse for wear backstage at some American theatre or other, Webb collided with a similarly over-refreshed Richard Harris, who proceeded to lead him in a round of bleary Irish songs. Several weeks later, and entirely out of the blue, Webb received a telegram which read, 'Dear Jimmy. Come to London. We'll make record. Richard.' It was to be Webb's first trip abroad.

'I arrived in London, I would say, in its heyday – teeming with celebrities. I had a knapsack full of cash and entrée almost anywhere I wanted to go. Richard and I proceeded to have ourselves a high old time. Life was a great deal of fun around Mr Harris, and I don't know anyone who would deny that, except perhaps some of his ex-wives.'

And somewhere in the middle of the fooling around, they managed an album, called *A Tramp Shining*, in which the rich-voiced Harris took a shot at a seven-minutes-and-twenty-seconds-long experimental piece entitled 'MacArthur Park.' Much later, Donna Summer would froth this up disco-style, much to the amazement of Webb who 'did not consider it had any commercial possibilities whatsoever'. Since then, enough people have ripped into its whimsical lyrics ('Someone left the cake out in the rain', etc, etc.) and Webb sounds, frankly, tired of talking about it. 'I wrote it about meeting a girlfriend in her lunchbreaks in LA. I can't account for its phenomenal success. It's been recorded by everyone from the Four Tops to Waylon Jennings, just everybody. I'm on overkill with it. Weird Al Jankovic is doing a version of it now, with my permission, called 'Jurassic Park'. I don't think it's necessary for anyone to record it again. It's completely bewildering and it won't go away.'

Webb started flying to London regularly. He met the Beatles for the first time while they were making *The White Album*. 'The picture is very clear to me. Paul is sitting at the piano with a sweater tied around his neck, and Linda is sitting behind him at the same stool with her arms around him while he's playing. And on the other side of the studio is a rug laid out on the floor where John is sitting with Yoko. There are candles there, sort of like a little camp made on the floor. George is standing in the middle of the floor playing bass, for some reason. And Ringo is invisible because the drum booth is below the control room. You couldn't see him, but you could hear him wisecracking.

'After a while, Paul came into the booth and somebody introduced me as Tom Dowd of Atlantic Records. I was so paralysed with fear, I didn't correct them. So I'm introduced all round – 'George Martin, this is Tom Dowd – John, Tom Dowd. And I'm Paul McCartney, Tom.' They're doing playbacks and Paul is asking me, in my persona as Tom Dowd, what I think of these guitar overdubs they've done. I'm trying to be helpful, but I'm completely confused. But what I am is a victim of one of those classic Beatles send-up things which they used to do to everybody. It was like, Jimmy Webb's coming, let's have him on. If you were on their territory, you were fair game. After this had gone on for way too long. George came over and whispered in my ear, Hey, man, I really liked your arrangement for "MacArthur Park".'

So perhaps we should understand the following piece of odd paranoia which Webb, without so much as a flicker of irony, leans a little closer and confesses to. 'One night I was listening to "Hey Jude". It turns out that "Hey Jude" is seven minutes-twenty-one-seconds long – one second longer than "MacArthur Park!" It's more than strange. I think it was the Beatles having me on a little bit.'

The high times continued with Harry Nilsson. They were in London together during the making of *Nilsson Schmilsson*. 'Harry and I took a shot at destroying the town. We'd get some cocaine, get a Phantom V, get a couple of bottles of champagne, put them in an ice bucket, get in the Rolls, and see how much mischief we could get into. See how many girls would fit inside a Rolls-Royce Phantom V.

'When John was separated from Yoko that time, the phone rang at six in the morning and Harry said, You've to to do something for me. John and I got in a little trouble last night. We were at the Troubadour and we got in this row and this photographer claims that John took a punch at him. He's gonna sue John and I need a witness. They came over and picked me up, we rode down there, I went in and told his lawyer I'd seen the whole

Hated, then fired by Brian Wilson, his father (Murry Wilson, page 140) managed the Beach Boys almost from their inception, though he was always strictly against any kind of experimentation or musical exploration. In this respect he was not unlike Mike Love, or at least the Mike Love that used to be

thing, that John never touched him, lying through my teeth. But that was the code with John. Whatever was asked of you, you did.'

Webb says he calmed down a little when he got married in 1973. For seven years he flew gliders and neglected his career. He went through a stage of 'progressive responsiblity' with the arrival of children (he now has six, aged between twenty and two) and even gave up the gliders after the third. But not before forcing George Martin to record the sound of his plane making a low pass over the airfield for a track on Webb's own *El Mirage* album – one of the six solo albums he had made prior to *Suspending Disbelief*, produced by Linda Ronstadt. None of these has stormed the charts. As he puts it, 'I made six albums and sold six albums.'

In 1980, Webb moved in to this studio in New York, to be next to the musical producer Michael Bennett, on several of whose stage projects he was working. When Bennett died of AIDS, Webb stayed on, responded to commissions, got eighties hits away with Ronstadt and Art Garfunkel, put together a little solo club act of his own material, composed the songs for his new album. But in the back of his mind, there remained this one abiding memory . . .

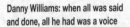

Danny Williams: when all was said and done, all he had was a voice

'I'm sitting at the piano, playing Sinatra things, and he's standing there in his bathrobe, glasses on, reading the sheet music, humming along. For a songwriter, this has to be pretty much the ultimate. And he turns to Frank Jr and says, "I think we can make a hit out of that, don't you?" It's unreal. But somehow, it's never come off.

'Still,' he adds, cracking a broad smile, 'to be able to hang out with these people? Life shouldn't be so good.'
(First published in *Q*, 1994.)

classic

Danny Williams
'Moon River' (2.31)
Single (HMV) 1961
To paraphrase Frank Sinatra, forget Audrey Hepburn and Henry Mancini, the best version of the *Breakfast At Tiffany's* theme is by this silky-voiced South African. Listening was never so smooth, or so easy.

classic

Murry Wilson

'The Warmth Of The Sun' (2.13)
Album: The Many Moods Of Murry Wilson (Capital) 1967
Jealous of his sons' success, the father of Brian, Dennis and Carl Wilson released this largely self-penned and self-produced LP. It also includes this rather grandiose version of one of Brian's most endearing tunes.

classic

Helmut Zacharias

'Tokyo Melody' (3.06)
Single (Polydor) 1964
A German orchestra, an Eastern bop. Still a very strange, deceptive record.

The Zither

Aside from the relentless duelling banjos of *Deliverance,* no other instrument has been so closely associated with a film as the zither playing 'The Harry Lime Theme' in Carol Reed's 1949 tip-top noir, *The Third Man.* Orson Welles never looked so enigmatic, Vienna never felt so forbidding, and the zither never seemed so cloying. *Bown bu-bown bu-bown bu-boowwn,* as they say in Austria.

Goodnight . . .

Above: Space agent Helmut Zacharias produced dozens of generic, sepia-tinted travelogues

Right: Anton Karas's solo zither score for Carol Reed's justly celebrated 1949 noir lends *The Third Man* an an all-too-predictable but no less disturbing edge, one exploited fully by the movie's other star, Orson Welles

The Index

Picture acknowledgements

Illustrations ©: All Action/Simon Meaker p17; A.J. Barratt p24 (top); BBC p104 (bottom); Brad Branson p91 (centre); Hannah Bryan p118; Lynn Goldsmith p49 (right); Mike Lipscombe p119; London Features International pp48, 69 (right), 79 (right), 84, 87 (bottom), 92 (top & bottom right), 99 (top), 103, 120, /Curt Gunther 79 (right), /Harry Hammond p56, /Bob Willoughby/Motion Picture and Television Photo Archive p89 (right); HHCL and Westbay Distributors Ltd p74 (bottom); Gen Inaba p85; Don Paulsen/Michael Ochs Archives/Venice, CA p46; Pearl & Dean p24 (bottom); Pictorial Press Ltd p135; Redferns pp51, 138, /Glenn A. Baker Archives pp45, 89 (left), /Colin Fuller p55 (left), /Gems pp37, 49 (left), /Richard Howells p139, /Michel Linssen 100 (bottom), /Michael Ochs Archives 19, 43, 58, 60, 74 (top), 86 (top), 93 (bottom), 101, 104 (top), 114, /David Redfern 26, 69 (left), 70, 76–7, 125, /Des Willie 50; Ronald Grant Archive pp54, 82, 100 (top), 102 (top), 140 (bottom); Einar Snorri p47; Topham p16.